#2

BURDY

Advance Praise for *Burdy*

Whenever I read Karen Spears Zacharias, I am struck by the disarming and haunting purity of a child's voice—as if Scout is alive and writing books. Zacharias' sophomore novel, *Burdy*, is a tender and moving story following broken people who mend equally broken people with the messy glue of mankind—love. Maybe Zacharias can write about the ripple effects of "men and their damn wars" because she's lived through them, heard the doorbell ring, and still got the telegram to prove it. Maybe her words bubble up and out of a heart held together by the same glue. Whatever the source, her authenticity is inviting, and her honesty is brazen and unashamed. Her voice echoes well beyond the last page.

> —Charles Martin, *New York Times* bestselling
> author of *Water from My Heart* and *A Life Intercepted*

Karen Spears Zacharias' new novel offers a full strength dose of reading joy. Tough and warm, sly and wise, *Burdy* demands a single sitting read. Prepare to be captivated.

> —Karen Karbo, author of
> *Julia Child Rules: Lessons on Savoring Life*

Karen Spears Zacharias' new novel *Burdy* takes us back to the Appalachia of East Tennessee that we visited in *Mother of Rain*, into the world of mountain coves and isolated communities, the world of Melungeon healers and visions and long-kept secrets. Zacharias' prose sings with tumbling rivers and forested hilltops, with the pain and loss of war, suicide, grief and guilt, and with the joys of connection, community, love, and the relief that comes when we know the truth. Books clubs will love spending time with *Burdy*, a one-of-a-kind original from the hand of a master.

> —Taylor M. Polites, author of *The Rebel Wife*

The crack of gunshots in a small Tennessee town ignites a lost tale that finds Burdy Luttrell leaving her home in the holler to travel to France on the trail of long-buried family secrets. In prose as clear as spring water and as lyrical as an old-time reel, Zacharias explores the lengths people are willing to go to bury the past and the emotional pitfalls of getting down in the dirt and digging it up.

> —Wiley Cash, *New York Times* bestselling author of
> *This Dark Road to Mercy* and *A Land More Kind Than Home*

Burdy

A Novel

Karen Spears Zacharias

Mercer University Press | MACON, GEORGIA

MUP/ P514

© 2015 by Karen Spears Zacharias
Published by Mercer University Press
1400 Coleman Avenue
Macon, Georgia 31207
9 8 7 6 5 4 3 2 1

Books published by Mercer University Press are printed on acid-
free paper that meets the requirements of the American National
Standard for Information Sciences—Permanence of Paper for
Printed Library Materials.

ISBN 978-0-88146-556-3
Cataloging-in-Publication Data is available from the Library of
Congress

It is love alone that counts

—St. Thérèse de Lisieux

Previous Work

Mother of Rain: A Novel

Karly Sheehan: The True Crime Story behind Karly's Law

Will Jesus Buy Me a Double-wide? ('Cause I Need More Room for My

Plasma TV)

Where's Your Jesus Now? Exploring How Fear Erodes Our Faith

After the Flag Has Been Folded: A Daughter Remembers the Father She

Lost to War

Benched: The Memoirs of Judge Rufe McCombs

Beloved,

who has stood beside me,

On the beaches at Normandy,

The hills of Tennessee,

The valleys of Oregon,

And at the Wall in D.C.,

For you

MERCER
UNIVERSITY PRESS

Endowed by
TOM WATSON BROWN
and
THE WATSON-BROWN FOUNDATION, INC.

Part I

1987

Chapter 1

Burdy didn't set out that morning aiming to get shot by the end of the day. But it was the cause of her wondering if Creator God hadn't up and moved off the mountain to a whole new place, like a Yankee retiree relocating to Seaside, Florida. Some TV preachers liked to say God was put out with his people, his chosen people. Given all Burdy came to bear witness to, she could hardly blame Creator if he walked out on the whole lot of humanity and never looked back.

Dr. O'Connor was the trauma surgeon on duty at the University of Tennessee Medical Center when Burdy arrived that Thursday evening in late September 1987. She was in surgery for several hours. Later, in the recovery room, Burdy's eyes fluttered whenever anyone called out her name.

"We are going to continue to monitor you for the next 24 hours," Dr. O'Connor said. "I'm hoping we can save your leg, Mrs. Luttrell."

"That's good news, huh, Mrs. Luttrell?" a recovery room nurse asked.

Burdy did not consider getting shot at any kind of good news at all. She didn't respond to the question. She couldn't. Burdy's tongue was limp. Spit pooled at the back of her throat, ran out the side of her mouth.

From that first moment when she was shot, a calm had come over Burdy like the time she fell backwards in the church aisle, slain in the Spirit. She'd gone down lickety-split when that visiting preacher put his index finger to her forehead. She did not fall back with the thud one might expect from somebody as short and squat as her. No, Burdy fell gentle like a dove feather.

The morphine overcame her now. She heard the monitors beeping, the whoosh-whoosh of machines, a phone ringing far off, and the doctor carrying on about whether he ought to go ahead and saw off her leg, but Burdy couldn't rise up, couldn't raise a finger in protest. She could only lay there mute, waiting on the Lord God to either revive her to this world or take her to the other.

"I'll be back by in the morning," Dr. O'Connor said. "Meanwhile, these nurses are going to take good care of you." Pausing in the doorway, he said, "You really are a very lucky woman, Mrs. Luttrell."

If Burdy could have reached the vase of overpriced hothouse flowers sitting beside her bed, she would have thrown it at Dr. O'Connor's wide head. It don't matter where you're from or who your people are, it is not your lucky day when a hollerin' man points a gun in your face. Burdy could attest to that.

She had been meaning to tell Rain about the letters that started arriving at her place years after Maizee died. In her mind, she'd had the conversation with him a thousand different times, but each time it ended badly. So Burdy kept putting it off the way some people do an abscessed tooth, fooling themselves into thinking it'll get better if they ignore it long enough, but it never does.

The day Rain turned twelve, he had written Burdy a note: "When I grow up, I'm going across the big pond and find out what happened to my daddy." Burdy didn't doubt for one minute that Rain would do it.

She always knew Rain would never come back to the Bend once he left. At least not for any long stretch of time. The Bend held too many painful memories for him. Whenever he went into Rogersville, he crossed the stretch of river where his momma was found dead. He couldn't even go to church at the Bend without laying eyes on his parents' headstones in the graveyard.

Burdy had summoned Rain from her hospital bed, saying it was important that she see him as soon as possible.

He had known nothing of any secret letters belonging to Burdy when he booked an early-morning flight to Knoxville. He only knew that he had to get home as quick as possible. After leaving Dr. Singh and the gathering at Rosecliff, Rain had returned to his hotel room and placed a call to Wheedin via the teletype.

"It's Momma," Wheedin said. "She's been shot. Come quick."

Chapter 2

The call distracted Rain. He was walking across the lawn at Rosecliff when a waiter brought him a note that said a Miss Wheedin
Luttrell needed him to call her as soon as possible. Rain slipped the
note into the pocket of his suit coat and continued to give polite
attention to his companion. Dr. Singh was one of the featured
panelists for an annual fundraiser scheduled later that day at Rhode
Island's historic Rosecliff mansion. Dr. Singh was detailing critical
advances in the deaf community, specifically cochlear implants.

"This will give the deaf greater mobility," Dr. Singh said.
"And, more importantly, greater independence." The doctor knew
that Rain valued independence.

Rain listened politely, relying primarily on the oral skills of lip
reading he learned at the Tennessee School for the Deaf. Lip
reading and the use of an amplified hearing aid allowed him to
transition between the deaf and hearing communities with relative
ease. He was not a proponent of cochlear implants, something Dr.
Singh also knew.

"Please excuse me a moment," Rain said. His speech was mostly understandable, especially to an attentive listener, but he always
signed as well. It was his way of making sure he was understood.

"Of course," Dr. Singh said. Singh turned to accept a glass of
merlot offered by one of a dozen slim-hipped waiters serving the
crowd that had gathered in the gardens.

Rain lifted his eyes and looked out across the grassy carpet.
Every emerald blade was cut so crisply that Rain imagined a dozen
barbers in red aprons down on their knees, sharpened scissors in
hand, clipping away. The waters of Narragansett Bay were calm, too
calm. Why hadn't he noticed that before?

Still waters back home meant something gone bad wrong. Usually, some chemical had leaked into the river from up Kingsport way and raised the water temperature, threatening to kill everything living beneath the surface. Rain hadn't been old enough to see what happened to the Holston after the TVA put in all those dams, but he'd paid attention to the stories Burdy and Leela-Ma would tell about how the river swallowed down whole communities, washing back courthouses and graves in one silent gulp.

Wheedin calling Rain wasn't out of the ordinary. While she had never returned to Christian Bend to live, Wheedin took great strides to be a part of Rain's life. Early on, she had been the one to make sure he got the best education available to a deaf child. It was at Wheedin's insistence that Leela-Ma and Burdy finally agreed to send Rain off to Knoxville to attend Tennessee's School for the Deaf. Oh, how those two had fought her on that! Neither woman wanted Rain anywhere out of their sight. After his momma died, Leela-Ma and Burdy had hovered over him like emissaries of God, which, truth be told, they both figured themselves to be.

Even now, all these years later, Rain could not think of his momma without a familiar longing, the hurt spilling out like hot coffee, burning from the inside out.

He walked past the caterer's tent, nodding at familiar faces, past the grand pool filled with floating magnolias flown in from Atlanta the day before. He walked away from the crowd, staring off into the bay waters as if he were looking for a boat, a sail, a dark cloud gathering. But all he saw for miles and miles was still water.

Chapter 3

Rain settled into seat 3-B and exhaled a sigh of gratitude for being seated on the aisle. While the pretty Delta stewardess explained how to lock a seatbelt, Rain reached for a newspaper somebody from the previous flight had left in the backseat pocket. Searching Sunday's *Knoxville News Sentinel*, Rain found the headline story just below the fold:

> BEAN STATION—Three people are dead and one other victim remains in critical condition at the University of Tennessee Medical Center following a shooting Thursday afternoon at the Laidlow Pharmacy in Bean Station.
>
> Police Chief Pleasant Conley said that at approximately 2:52 p.m. a person wearing camouflage gear entered the store and walked straight back to the pharmacy counter.
>
> "Customers reported seeing a holstered gun, but a person with a gun is not unusual around these parts," Chief Conley said.
>
> Especially not during hunting season. "And it is hunting season around here every day of the year," said customer Paul Purdy, who exited the store as the gunman entered. "I come down to pick up some Anacin for mother. She got the arthritis bad. It's the only thing that she'll take for the pain. I was in and out. Glad I was too, when I heared what happened to the others."
>
> Chief Conley said the gunman ordered the pharmacy clerk and customers back behind the counter.

Names of the deceased victims are being withheld until next-of-kin have been notified. Burdy Luttrell, of Christian Bend, is the lone survivor of the shooting spree. She remains in critical but stable condition, authorities at University of Tennessee Medical Center confirmed.

Laidlow Pharmacy of all places. Kade Mashburn, a good friend of Rain's dead momma, had taken Rain there once. They had sat at the lunch counter, ordered grilled cheese sandwiches and thick vanilla shakes. Kade was working on learning sign language. He wasn't proficient but he was passable.

The two had talked history and fishing holes. After lunch, they rode up to the Clinch River Overlook. Kade told Rain about the hunters who traveled the crossroads near Bean Station in search of furs to sell, and about how all that fur trading turned the town into a center of commerce. A lot of changes had come to the mountains since Rain went off up North, but Bean Station remained a wide spot in the road with a long and celebrated history.

Doc Lawson was the closet thing to a father Rain knew. Doc had tried his best to learn to sign but gave up on it in a fit of frustration. He could never master it as well as Kade. So Doc relied on Rain to lip-read, and they made out alright.

Hearing aids had helped Rain a great deal. And it also helped that he wasn't born deaf. He could hear just fine until the bad fever that had ruptured his left eardrum and rendered him deaf. By the time he started school, some of his hearing was restored. He could hear horns blowing or the muffled sounds of people talking, but he could not hear the whisper of the wind or the whoosh of his own footsteps. Crowds were still difficult to manage, especially with the hearing devices. All that noise at once, coming from all different directions like Knoxville traffic, had a way of jamming everything up.

Rain was nineteen, in his freshman-year studies at Gallaudet University in D.C., when he read about the work of Dr. William House. The Oregon doctor made headlines with the first cochlear implant in 1961. It was rudimentary, and there were fears that implanting such a device might fry the eardrums altogether, but House was not dissuaded. Gallaudet was rife with debate over what the advances might mean for the deaf community. Rain dreamed of the day when he could stand at the base of Horseshoe Falls and feel—and hear—the water thunder over the cliffs.

Without telling anyone, not Kade or even Wheedin, Rain had contacted Dr. House and volunteered to be one of his test patients. House suggested that Rain wait a few years, until he was out of college. But those years on his own at college made him self-sufficient, and by the time his graduation date approached, he had abandoned the idea of cochlear implants. Rain figured that, in many ways, his deafness was his strength. It was the thing that informed his life choices, made him the man he was becoming.

During his senior year at Gallaudet University, Rain worked as an intern for Luther Holcomb, the vice-chair of the newly formed Equal Employment Opportunity Commission. Before Rain accepted his college diploma in June 1966, Holcomb offered the boy from Christian Bend a full-time position on his staff.

Kade and Wheedin made the trip to D.C. for the graduation. Leela-Ma and Doc refused to attend, no matter how much Rain pleaded. As far as he knew, neither of them had been further north than Abingdon, Virginia, about an hour's drive from home. He was glad to have the other two, even if they were much fewer in number than those who'd attended his high school graduation, all of them there to celebrate the deaf boy who had achieved valedictorian status and earned a Presidential scholarship to Gallaudet.

Not that Leela-Ma had been in favor of Rain heading off to Yankee territory. She wasn't the least bit keen on him going so far away. She'd hoped he would come back to the mountain and farm

10

for the Moselys or maybe work as a foreman on Paddy Christian's property. Paddy owned half the mountain, and he'd taken a real shine to Rain during the summers Rain had worked for him. Paddy didn't have any boys of his own to deed the farm to, and Leela-Ma was sure that if Rain wanted a farm of his own, Paddy would make it happen.

Chapter 4

Wheedin hit the call button. She hadn't left her Momma's side since arriving at the Knoxville hospital late Thursday night. By the time Wheedin made the drive from her home in Columbia, South Carolina, Burdy had already been through surgery and was in the recovery room. Burdy had slept most of Saturday and a good bit of Sunday morning. Here it was nearly one o'clock Sunday afternoon, and Burdy could not be roused. Wheedin was no nurse, but with one look at her mother today she knew that something bad was going on. Burdy's face was flushed. Sweat beaded on her forehead and in the softness of her neck folds. Wheedin touched her mother's forearm and felt sticky, clammy skin, as if Burdy had been push-mowing the yard on a summer's day.

"Momma?" Wheedin said, leaning over the bed. "Momma? Can you hear me?"

Burdy did not respond.

The dinner cart clanged in the hallway. An orderly parked it right outside Room 204. Wheedin pushed the call button again, looking across the bed to the IV dripping pain medication into her mother's veins. Rain had sent a message saying he'd arrive in Knoxville on the five o'clock flight out of Providence. He'd pick up a rental car and be on his way. Five o'clock couldn't come soon enough for Wheedin.

Nurse Collins stepped around the orderly and into Burdy's room.

"Something's the matter," Wheedin said. "I can't rouse Momma. I think she might have a fever."

The yellow-haired nurse shoved aside the bedside tray, checked the IV line, then leaned over the bed rail and called out, "Mrs. Luttrell? Mrs. Luttrell!"

Burdy remained still and silent. Nurse Collins took out her stethoscope and pressed it to Burdy's chest, taking note that her breathing had grown shallow. She threw back the covers, pushed Burdy's hospital gown up.

Wheedin gasped. A dirty fluid seeped out from around the bandage that covered the thigh wound. Blisters had formed around the rim of the bandage.

Nurse Collins reached for the call button, panic flashing behind her dark eyes.

Chapter 5

No one was in Room 204 when Rain arrived. The bed covers were tossed back. A well-worn copy of *Trees of Heaven* rested in a chair. Rain recognized it as Wheedin's book.

He walked to the window and looked out across the hospital parking lot. An orange and white University of Tennessee flag flapped from the antenna of a pickup circling the lot. Rain had long followed UT's sports but was glad he'd missed yesterday's game-day traffic.

"Rain?"

He felt a hand on his shoulder. Turning from the window, he looked into the face of the woman who had been his mother's best childhood friend. Embracing her, Rain said nothing as sobs shook her body.

It wasn't like Wheedin to be so emotional. Rain rubbed her back, wondering if he'd misunderstood her earlier. She'd said that Burdy was badly injured, but compared to the ones killed, she had faired well enough. The bullet had torn through her upper thigh. Though the wound was serious, the trauma surgeon had reassured Wheedin that it wasn't life threatening. Her momma would be okay. At least that's the word Rain received. Why was Wheedin so upset?

A fire-headed girl wearing a pink-and-white uniform walked into the room carrying bedding. Her nametag read *Loretta*. "Oh, I'm sorry," she said. "I can come back later. I was just going to change the sheets."

For a split second Rain wondered if Burdy might never come back to that room—or to any room. It felt like somebody had taken a branding iron to his chest. Was he too late?

14

Wheedin pulled away, grabbed tissues from Kleenex box, and blew her nose. "No, it's okay. Go ahead," she said. "Momma is in surgery."

"If you're sure, ma'am. I don't want to be a bother. I'll be real fast. I promise," Loretta said. "I'm the fastest bed-maker in the entire hospital. I was named volunteer of the month last week."

"You don't say," said Wheedin. Her eyelashes were wet as she smiled up at Rain.

"Oh, yes, ma'am," Loretta said, yanking the sheets from the bed. "I've been volunteering here longer than any other Candy Striper. Going on four years now. I started the summer before my freshman year of high school and I'm a senior now. I'm graduating in May." She tossed the dirty sheets on the floor and wiped down the bed rails with a disinfectant that made the entire room smell.

"I've already been accepted at UT. They even gave me an award. It covers my tuition for four years," she informed them, snapping a clean sheet across the mattress. "'Course, I have to keep my grades up, but I will!"

"I'm sure you will," Wheedin said. She walked to the garbage can and threw away the tissues, then checked her face in the mirror above the sink. It was unmarked, owing to the fact that she rarely wore makeup. With the blessing of her Melungeon complexion, she didn't need it.

Loretta was still rambling. Rain wasn't sure how she managed to get enough breath to work.

"I am a good student," she was saying as she stuffed a pillow into a clean pillowcase. "I'm going to study to be a geneticist. You know, a blood historian."

"A blood historian?" Wheedin asked.

"Well," Loretta said, laughing, "kinda. That's how I think of it, anyway. Yeah, see my father died when I was a little girl."

"I'm sorry," Wheedin said.

"No, it's okay. I mean, no, it wasn't okay. I mean I'm okay now. But he died from a blood disease when I was five. Doctors told Momma that the disease was genetic. I'm the only child, and we don't know if I'll get the disease or not. But I figure if I become a geneticist, maybe I can help find a cure."

"Sounds like a good plan," Wheedin said.

"Well, there!" Loretta said, picking up the dirty sheets off the floor. "Told you I would be quick. Mrs. Luttrell's bed is all clean and ready for her when she returns from surgery. Now if you'll excuse me, please. I have more beds to change." With a smile, she backed herself out of the room and took off lickety-split down the hall, cradling dirty laundry.

Rain looked at Wheedin. "Surgery?" he signed.

"I was trying to tell you," Wheedin said. "Momma has some sort of infection. They rushed her back to surgery. Said if they didn't get ahead of it now, she might lose more than a leg."

Chapter 6

A couple of members of the UT surgical team could recite the name of the patient stretched out before them. Others knew only her age, blood pressure, and heart rate. Dr. Barnes, the general surgeon, knew that the woman was stronger than her years would suggest.

He noted that for a woman of eighty, Burdy's muscle tone was taut. Probably a farmer's wife, he figured. Used to outdoor work. The gunshot had shattered her right thigh and nicked the femoral artery. She'd definitely have to take a break from hard labor.

"There aren't too many survivors of triple homicides," Barnes said as he leaned in to better inspect Burdy's infected wound. His dry humor confused his surgical staff, but it amused him.

Dr. Barnes had not treated Burdy when she first arrived at the hospital. The trauma surgeon had seen to her. Still, Barnes knew what others on staff were only beginning to suspect. Dr. O'Connor, once one of the finest surgeons in the region, had a reckless lifestyle that was beginning to take its toll. While Barnes couldn't say for sure that O'Connor's sloppy work had led to the infection that now raged through the patient's body, Barnes had his concerns.

The patient's Melungeon background meant nothing to the doctor. Burdy's chart simply read "Bi-racial." Dr. Barnes had grown up in white-washed Kirkland, Washington. Until his move to Tennessee three years prior, he knew racial tensions only as historical fact, something he'd read about from time to time. He had a high school teacher who insisted on reading Martin Luther King, Jr.'s *Letter from a Birmingham Jail* once a year, but Barnes had marked that up to typical English teacher eccentricity. He could not have found Sneedville or Newman's Ridge with a map, a compass, and a guide dog.

The first time he heard the story of the elephant hanging in Erwin, Barnes was sitting at a dinner party in a fancy home along Lyons View. He'd responded by laughing, thinking that the hostess, a pinch-nosed Birmingham transplant, was repeating some lame myth she'd heard from the locals. "Who but a Southerner would think to hang an elephant?" he'd bellowed.

Only afterwards, when no one laughed along with him, did Barnes realize that it was no joke. The people in Erwin really had hung an elephant named Mary. He was so mortified by the discovery that he avoided the hostess and her husband thereafter, refusing all invitations to socialize with them again.

Barnes wasn't at all sure he could save the patient's leg, but he was determined to try. "It's staph," he proclaimed. "We'll have to go deep. Scalpel, please."

Chapter 7

Burdy spent the next few nights in ICU, feverish and delirious. Rain and Wheedin took turns sitting bedside, feeding Burdy bits of ice, wiping her forehead, her face, and her neck with a cold cloth. They slept fitfully in straight-back chairs, waking suddenly to watch the IV drip and listen for her shallow breaths over the beep of heart and oxygen monitors.

Each morning before the nurse shift change, Rain would slip his stocking feet into black-leather loafers and head out to the do-nut shop around the corner. There he purchased two large cups of steaming coffee and two fried apple turnovers from Henry, who wore a UT cap squashed down on his head, his black hair spread out over his ears like starling wings.

Despite having Wheedin's breakfast in hand, Rain never hurried back. These walks were his only chance to be outside. He appreciated the early mist that fell over Knoxville, and he breathed deep the sweet morning air drifting from the mountains over the river.

One of those mornings, he sat on a bench directly beyond the merry-go-round door that spilled people in and out of the hospital. A black woman wearing thick white shoes and a top printed with pink-and-green lollipops walked past and smiled. Rain nodded and took a sip of his coffee. Leela-Ma used to keep a cross-stitch pillow on her rocking chair that read, "A smile first thing in the morning can set the rest of the day right." He figured it was true.

Seeing a discarded newspaper, Rain scanned through the headlines. Was it Tuesday already? Hospitals are the vortex where time warps. Taking the warm apple turnover from the brown paper poke, Rain ate it down in three bites, washing it back with the black coffee.

Burdy used to make him apple turnovers whenever he came home on school break. She'd pick the apples about this same time of year, core, peel, and slice them. Then she'd lay them out flat on wax paper that covered her buffet, which she pushed up close to the big picture window in her living room. She'd cover the sliced apples with paper towels and leave them there to dry in the sunshine for days. Maybe a week or two. Her turnovers beat Henry's any day.

Rain never did learn to how to cook like Burdy or Leela-Ma. Actually, there were a lot of things about life in Christian Bend that he hadn't learned. He hadn't wanted to. Once he had the chance to get away, he'd left without looking back.

But now, sitting on the bench outside the Medical Center and finishing his last gulp of coffee, Rain wondered if maybe he had walked away from the very thing he'd been chasing all these years since, a chance at belonging to somebody. Burdy had warned him about that more than once.

"That thing you are aching for, Rain, it can't be found anywhere else except right here," she'd said. "These mountains cradle the bones of your ancestors. They'll cradle your bones one day, too. No matter how far off you go, no matter how many places you call home, you will never be able to replace the Bend."

When he left for D.C., Rain had told Burdy he wasn't looking to replace Christian Bend as much as he was looking to escape it. "I don't want to live in the shadow of these mountains," he said. "I don't mean to be disrespectful, Burdy, but you don't understand. Christian Bend holds a lot of painful memories for me. Well, not even memories, really, as much as the absence of them. It's hard to grow up in a place where everyone but you knows your parents."

Rain remembered how Burdy rose up from the davenport. She'd walked into the kitchen and straight out the back door without saying anything. Nothing. Just up and walked out of her house and left him standing there.

He followed her, found her at the edge of the yard in the shadow of the hillside. Towering over her, he put his arms around her from behind and pulled her close to his strong chest. He rested his chin on her wiry gray head. She placed her stubby and weathered hands over his tanned forearms.

"I love you, Rain."

That was all she had said, wrapped in Rain as a tear fell from her cheek onto his arm.

When Rain got back to the ICU, Dr. Barnes was talking with Wheedin. Handing her the lukewarm coffee and pastry, Rain mumbled an apology.

"Sorry I was gone so long."

"It's okay." Wheedin put the paper poke aside. "Dr. Barnes was just giving me an update on Momma. They're going to move her out of ICU today."

"That's great!" Rain said. Then he looked over at Dr. Barnes. "Right?"

Barnes was cautious with his answer. Rain watched him carefully. He didn't want to miss any of the doctor's words.

"To be quite honest, staph is a very serious infection. I had to cut much further into the thigh muscle than I'd hoped. We'll have to wait and see how Mrs. Luttrell responds. We have to take this one day at a time for now."

Rain looked over at Wheedin, who was looking at her momma. Burdy was pitiful, lying there with an IV running through a thick vein, her long hair braided, more white than gray now, her skin more gray than brown. Never before had she seemed so frail and so old, so unlike herself.

Chapter 8

At the old brick police station on the corner of Main and Third, Chief Conley leaned back in his chair and pushed a button on the speakerphone. "Darlene, hold all my calls, please. I do not want to be interrupted. I don't care if President Clinton is calling."

"Okay, but you got my message that Governor McWherter called?"

"Yes, got it."

"He said whatever help you need, it's yours."

"I'm going to hold him to that."

Switching off the speaker, Conley looked across the metal desk at Detective Wiley. Wiley's orange hair was washing away to white at his temples. Seeing age on his pal made Conley wince. He had a few years on Wiley, but still. It was hard to see friends getting older. Conley was thankful he'd gone bald in his twenties. It took the pressure off aging.

"I'm hoping that means the forensics are gonna be fast-tracked," Wiley said.

"McWherter don't make many promises he can't keep," Conley assured him.

A triple homicide was the last thing Chief Conley wanted to deal with. He was only six months away from retirement. But the Laidlow shooting was the biggest crime to hit Bean Station in his thirty-four-year career, and he was stuck with it.

"Tell me what you have on this fellow," he said.

"Well, first off, we don't know for sure it was a fellow," Wiley said.

Conley pulled a Marlboro pack from his shirt pocket and tapped a cigarette on his desk. "What makes you say that?" he asked.

"Facts." Wiley wrinkled his nose. He hated it when the Chief smoked, hated the way the tobacco smell sank into his clothes, the wood of his desk, the very walls of the office. "All we know about the shooter is that he was covered head to toe in camo gear: hat, shirt, pants, boots. Hell, Chief, just because the folks at Laidlow think they saw a man carrying the gun doesn't mean it was a man. Maybe it was a big-boned woman with her hair cut short or tucked up underneath a camo cap."

"Alright. What else you got?"

"Whoever it is has a hankering for hoarhound and meth."

"Hoarhound?"

"Yeah. That hard candy that tastes like root beer."

"I know what hoarhound is." Conley leaned forward on his elbows and took a drag, blowing smoke out the side of his mouth and upwards. Wiley watched it dissipate into the yellowing film that covered the plywood walls. He figured they would have to tear down the entire building to get rid of the smell of stale smoke and overcooked turnips from Minnie's Diner.

Wiley's eyes wandered around the room and landed on a couple of framed newspaper articles. The bold headlines and fine print detailed the only other high-profile murder cases he'd seen in his long years on the force. In the first, Ottechree Mason shot and killed his wife Vechel for running around on him. Nobody blamed Ottechree. Vechel was the town slut, but Ottechree kept right on loving that woman until the moment he caught her in bed with Ronnie Carson, the fifteen-year-old neighbor boy, and shot her dead. Ronnie ran home, got his daddy's rifle, and came back to shoot Ottechree dead.

Poor Ronnie. When Wiley brought him in for questioning, he didn't have the good sense to even try to deny what he'd done. He had mustered up every ounce of his 135 pounds and proudly told Wiley how much he had loved Vechel. In the middle of his confession, he broke down bawling like a boy who'd struck out in a playoff game. And that's what Ronnie was: a boy. But they charged him as a man and sentenced him to forty-five years in prison. The lives of two fellows wasted over a woman. Wiley shook his head, remembering. As far as he was concerned, the only good thing about those killings was all the men who'd be spared the lubricious ways of Vechel Mason.

"Did you hear me, Wiley?" Conley dropped his cigarette butt into a half-drunk, day-old bottle of RC Cola.

"Naw, sorry, boss."

"You're drifting, Wiley. I asked how you knew that the suspect liked hoarhound?"

"'Cause the shooter picked up three bags of it on his way out the door at Laidlow's. Didn't even bother checking the front register for cash. Took all the cash from the back, along with as many uppers as he could fit in that tote bag he was carrying. Wiped them out of amphetamines, too."

"Anyone happen to get the plates?" Conley asked. He rose up, tucked his shirt in tightly at the back, then picked up his holster and slipped it back on.

"Last two only—BL," Wiley said.

"You sure?" Conley asked.

"Not really," Wiley admitted. "Miss Bernadette swears she seen the plates on a silver vehicle speeding around the bend at Thorn Hill Gap. Said she was walking out to get the mail and the driver near about run her down. 'Course, Miss Bernadette is blind in one eye and can't see out the other, so who knows?"

"We get make and model on the car?"

"Yeah. New Jeep Cherokee. Silver."

"You get that from Miss Bernadette too?" Conley walked around the front of the desk.

24

"No. We got that from Paul Purdy, who said he'd seen it parked in the alley next to Laidlow and wondered who had the new rig." Wiley followed Conley as he headed out the door. "Where we going, Boss?"

"For a drive," Conley said.

Looking back later, Sheriff Conley would wonder why the Silver Jeep Cherokee didn't register with him that day.

As he later told the jurors, it just didn't, that's all.

Chapter 9

It had been one week since Burdy Luttrell stopped by Laidlow Drugstore in Bean Station to buy a birthday card for Leela. Until that brief but fateful stop, it was a good day.

Burdy and Mayne Hill had driven up to Lincoln Memorial University early that morning so Burdy could take a class on healing roots. Mayne agreed to drive her to Harrogate if Burdy would buy lunch in Cumberland Gap.

When she realized she'd been practicing most of what they taught for many years, Burdy skipped out of class. She and Mayne drove through the Gap, marveling over the golden ginkos and the flaming maples. They ate lunch at the Gaphouse Diner. Burdy had the potato soup, and Mayne the chili, although she later told Burdy she wished she'd ordered the soup instead. The chili was too spicy. Both women enjoyed their time together until they stop at Bean Station.

The shooting at Laidlow was like any other murder. All of it could have been avoided. And it wasn't as if Burdy needed to shop there. She had a drawer full of generic cards in the buffet at home, but she wanted to get Leela an extra-special card for her eightieth birthday.

She and Leela hadn't always been friends, but they had put aside their differences and grown close in the years after Maizee's death. Grief bound them, but friendship rooted them. In time, laughter replaced the tears they had shed together. So, after cutting class at Lincoln and filling her belly at Gaphouse, Burdy asked Mayne to stop by the pharmacy so she could find the perfect card. Mayne readily complied, as she wanted to pick up some antacids after the spicy chili. It was another way the incident could have been avoided; if Mayne had eaten the potato soup, she might have talked Burdy into waiting until they got to Rogersville to shop for a card.

Leela and Doc drove in from Christian Bend Friday morning, after Burdy was settled into a private room. Every day since the shooting, Wheedin had called Leela with an update, but always urged her to wait to visit until Budy got a private room. "You won't be able to get in anyway," Wheedin had said. "The visiting policy in ICU is so strict." So, gritting her teeth, Leela had waited until the end of the week to make the drive.

After they found Burdy's room and hugged Wheedin and Rain, Doc held up a mason jar packed with a paste he'd made from tea tree oil and bee pollen.

"Try and put some of this around her wound when they change the bandages," he said.

"I'm not sure the staff will let me do that," Wheedin said, reaching for the jar.

"Well, if they won't let you, do it when they ain't a'looking," Doc reasoned.

Wheedin glanced at Rain, who had returned to his spot on a chair, sitting with his elbows on his knees and a copy of July's *Southern Living* in his hands, pretty much the only reading material in the room other than the Gideon Bible. As his dark bangs fell across his forehead, she noticed that his eyes were red-rimmed and weary. He shrugged at her as if to say, "What good does it do to argue? Just go with it."

"Thank you, Doc," Wheedin said. "I'll see what I can do."

"Any improvement?" Leela asked. She wandered over to the bed and gently touched Burdy's hand.

"Not much," Wheedin said. "She roused for a bit yesterday afternoon and again this morning, but she was talking out of her head. She didn't know who I was or who Rain was, or where she was at. She kept thinking she was in France."

"France?" Leela said, her eyebrows raised in surprise.

"Yeah. She was in a panic over missing the boat."

"Good Lord," Doc said. "Morphine'll do that to a person. Causes all kinds of delusions."

"Yes. We thought so, too," Wheedin said. "But Dr. Barnes weaned her off the morphine on Wednesday morning. He said there's a possibility that Momma might be suffering from anesthesia-induced dementia."

"My lands," Leela said. "What does that mean?" She gently smoothed a curl off Burdy's forehead.

"Apparently, some people have trouble rousing after being put under." Wheedin sat at the foot of her momma's bed and rubbed her fingers back and forth across the covers, like she was trying to straighten out the dog-eared corner of a book. "When they come to, they don't know where they are. It's a type of amnesia. Sometimes they forget the names of loved ones. Some forget whole sections of their lives. The confusion can be temporary, but sometimes it never goes away. Right now, with Momma, we just don't know. She hasn't been awake long enough for Dr. Barnes to make an assessment."

Wheedin looked at each of them in turn, then back at Burdy.

"The thing is," she began. Then she paused, inhaled, and dropped her head down on the hospital bed. "Momma doesn't know who she is."

28

Part II

1956

Chapter 10

The day the airmail letter first arrived, the oxeye daisies bordering the walk between the house and the mailbox bunched together as if whispering secrets to one another. An unsteady script declared that the letter was for Mrs. Burdy Luttrell, Christian Bend, Tennessee. The postmark read June 21, 1956, Bayeux, France.

The sun's shadow was crossing behind Con Hill when Burdy came dragging butt up the road that Friday evening. In the not too far-off, Burdy heard the strains of Johnny Wright picking out a tune. There wasn't a string instrument Johnny couldn't play—banjo, guitar, mandolin, dulcimer. Tibbis used to say, "Johnny could string fishing wire around a frying pan and make it sing like one of them harps." When Johnny wasn't picking songs, he was writing them. He'd even sold a handful to some recording company up North. And it was no wonder, with such catchy tunes. Burdy hummed along as she walked, breathing in the scent of white clover in between notes.

"Hey, Miz Luttrell!" Little Fern Campbell ran out from the step where she'd been sitting. She stood at the edge of the yard where it met the asphalt, not one toe over, just like her momma told her to.

"Good afternoon, Fern," Burdy said. She pulled a blue bandanna out of her bra and wiped her brow.

"You tired? You sure look it," Fern blurted out before Burdy had time to reply.

"Do I now?" Burdy said, laughing.

"Yes, ma'am," Fern said, too young to speak anything but the guileless truth.

"How's your momma? Did that burn on her hand heal up?"

"Yes, ma'am. She used that salve you give her and it's all better. She's been in the kitchen canning tomatoes all day. I helped her till she told me to get on outside and play, said she needed some peace and quiet."

Burdy laughed again. Fern Campbell had been talking since she was a year old and had hardly stopped for a breath in the seven years since. Burdy felt for her poor momma. It'd be like having a blue jay squawking at a person all day long.

Fern held up a mason jar in one hand and its tin lid in the other. "I'm hunting for lightning bugs."

"Well, I'll let you get back to it then, darling," Burdy said, giving Fern a pat atop her dark head.

The sky turned pink and lavender. It was nigh on dusk by the time Burdy pulled the mail from the box. She grabbed it by the handful and stuffed it up next to her ample bosom as she walked around the back of the house. The bees were feeding in the mint as Burdy pulled open the screen door and let it slam shut behind her.

It wasn't until an hour later, over a supper of reheated green beans, potato cakes, and a hunk of cornbread that Burdy finally started sifting through the mail. Tucked between solicitations from the hardware store and Donny's market was the airmail letter. Burdy recognized the handwriting right off as that of Zebulon Hurd.

Burdy hadn't been home when the mail arrived. She was downriver at Pressmen's Home, the campus for the International Printing Pressmen's Union. A stone's throw on the other side of Rogersville, Pressmen's had its very own tuberculosis hospital. Aside from the hospital, the little community had a chapel, a post office, and practically everything else a town ought to have.

Pressmen's was built in the mountains because those city doctors thought the air would be best for the pressmen suffering from TB. At the time, so many pressmen got tuberculosis that some thought maybe the ink they worked with all day long caused it. Burdy thought that might be true. But no matter what caused the sickness, she felt it was her duty to help where she could.

It had taken her a while to find something meaningful to do. After Maizee died in 1944 and Rain went off to the deaf school in Knoxville, Wheedin went on back to South Carolina, and Burdy found herself at loose ends. She had tried to do all the things she'd done before—planting the garden, rooting for cures, taking offerings up to the gravehouse, keeping the grass mowed, seeing to the chickens, and helping the families in the Bend when when any of them took ill. But none of it was the same after Maizee.

Still, it wasn't in Burdy's nature to give herself fully over to the mulligrubs. Her own momma had embroidered a pillow that leaned up against the back of the davenport in Burdy's front room: *Hard Work Won't Kill a Person Near as Quick as Worry Will.* Having to look day in and day out at those red threads pulled through the linen by her momma's worked-to-the-bone fingers gave Burdy the motivation she needed to put one squatty foot in front of the other.

It was Doc, Maizee's uncle, who had finally told Burdy about the need for extra hands up at Pressmen's. Lots of perfectly healthy people refused to go into the TB hospital, fearing that they too would catch the disease that turned men who'd once been strong as horses weak as worms. Burdy didn't give over to such foolishness herself. She understood that the gift of healing came with the burden to use it rightly.

After Doc's suggestion, she started going to Pressmen's shortly before Christmas. Every Monday and Friday, Burdy would walk downriver and catch the ferry across the Holston. Once she was on the other side of the river, Mayne Hill, the Pressmen's postmistress, would give her a ride.

Burdy always carried a big bag that she'd fashioned together from burlap, with wide strips of velvet for the handles. She packed it full of her special potions: bagamilly, black drawing salve, elderberry, mullein, sneezeweed—many of the roots and potions she kept stored in mason jars in the root cellar. She also carried along a jar of apple butter because it was easier to get the men to take the bitter roots if she mixed them with something sweet.

Some of the ailing wouldn't accept her healing potions at all, not wanting to be served by a half-breed like her. Burdy knew those men were sick with more than just tuberculosis—they were suffering from a suffocation of the spirit.

When she decided to take Doc's suggestion, she was glad to find that Dr. Jenkins welcomed her. He lost one of Pressmen's foremen to consumption and told Burdy that he could use whatever help she was willing to give. Because he'd grown up in Hawkins County, Dr. Jenkins wasn't dismissive of Burdy and her healing abilities. He had earned a medical degree from Vanderbilt, but he always said he was practicing medicine. He considered Burdy his equal in the art of practicing.

After a year of service at the hospital, Burdy figured she might go on to college and earn herself one of those degrees in holistic medicine. Without telling another soul, she'd sent off for a home-study program and earned her high school diploma. It arrived with the official gold seal signifying her achievement, along with the signature of the school president.

When it came in the mail, Burdy had gone to town and bought a plain black frame at the hardware store. She put the diploma inside that frame and wrapped it all in an old pillowcase embroidered by her granny. Then she put the bundle in the bottom of her dresser drawer, underneath her nightgowns. If people in the Bend found out, they might poke fun at her, so she kept her learning to herself.

Now, home from Pressmen's with a supper plate next to her, Burdy read the address on the airmail letter again. Surely this was a sorry prank, or else somebody had found Zeb's belongings and gone through them. Maybe somebody had pawned his things off to a second-hand store, and the store clerk was forwarding on a letter Zeb forgot to mail.

Either way, seeing his handwriting all these years later rattled Burdy. She clasped the letter between two trembling hands, studied the familiar, tightly hooked "B" and the narrow "y," then she pushed back from the table, stood, and slid the unopened letter into her apron pocket.

Chapter 11

In the twelve years since Maizee's death, there had been no word on Zebulon. It was like once his widow was dead, the Army didn't feel the need to bring what was left of Zeb back home. Whatever obligation they had toward the family didn't seem to matter. Rain hadn't been old enough to raise a ruckus about them returning his daddy's remains. Grown men had a difficult time tracking anything through the military. It would have been nigh impossible for a young boy like him.

After the war ended, the *Knoxville Sentinel* had printed a tally of the total number of U.S. servicemen listed as Missing-in-Action: nearly 79,000. And that was the last time Burdy saw Zebulon Hurd's name mentioned in the news. It wasn't like everybody at Christian Bend up and forgot that his coffin was empty. It's just that they felt powerless to do anything about getting him home. Now, here in her apron pocket, Burdy had a letter that came to her from beyond the grave.

She cleared away the supper dishes and put a bowl of scraps on the porch for Useless, the mutt that Wheedin up and left with her momma when she moved off to South Carolina. Most dogs wouldn't eat green beans or cornbread, but Useless was a yard dog, and there was nothing he wouldn't eat. As he gobbled the food, Burdy stood with her hands on her hips and glanced over at the house where Zeb and Maizee had lived.

It had remained dark and uninhabited since the day Doc found Maizee on the bank of the Holston River. Over the years, several people had asked Burdy about renting it, but she always refused them. It didn't feel right letting someone else occupy the house.

For the most part, everything was left like it was the day Maizee died. Leela and Doc had taken Rain's clothes and things. They also took back that doll Maizee had carried around with her all the time. Burdy hadn't seen that doll in years. What was it called again? Hatty? Something like that. But other than Rain's things and the doll, nothing was changed. Burdy didn't have to go in to picture it; she knew it all by heart. Dust covered the yellow curtains. Maizee's Blue Willow china was arranged neatly on the table, also covered in dust. The davenport was pushed up against the big picture window, the crocheted dollies on the armrest faded with age.

The ladder-back chair Burdy had sat in the night Rain got sick with the fever was tucked into the bedroom corner. Zeb's old work clothes hung in the closet. His boots, caked with dried mud from Shug Mosely's farm, sat beside the bed where he'd left them. His letters, penned at Cottesmore and other bases, were stuffed in the family Bible. The house smelled of unused kerosene and an overwhelming loneliness.

Burdy shook her head to clear it, pushing away the memories that threatened to overcome her. At the edge of the property, in the woods leading up to Horseshoe Falls, lightning bugs flickered to a silent sacred tune. Burdy regarded them as dance partners with the stars, each one following the movement of the other to a tune only they could hear, some sort of primitive ritual formed long before the interruption of man.

If she hadn't thrown out her last tin of snuff ten years ago, Burdy would take a dip right now for sure. Used to be, all the women at the Bend dipped. Burdy couldn't remember when it went out of fashion, couldn't even remember when she'd learned that term, "out of fashion." Not that she cared one whit about fitting in or what others thought of her. She quit dipping mostly because it got harder to find good quality snuff. Stores made more profit off cigarettes and chew than they did the powder variety.

For generations, folks at the Bend grew their own plots of tobacco. As little as ten rows of it could bring a person a wad of cash. But once folks figured out that marijuana was a better cash crop, they swapped out the tobacco for it.

Useless had finished his dinner and flopped down in a bare patch he'd made in the yard. Burdy leaned over a rusty metal chair under the porch light and wiped off the dust and grime with an old clout, wishing she could live as carefree as a dog. When it was at least cleaner than before, she sat in the cold chair and pulled the letter from her pocket. Flipping open her pocketknife, she sliced open the envelope. Her stomach couldn't have ached more if she'd swallowed a handful of marbles. A sense of dread came over her anytime she knew she was about to find out something she wasn't sure she wanted to know:

Burdy,

I have written this letter a thousand times in my head. This is the first time I've actually put the pen to paper. I don't yet know if I have the courage to drop this in the mail.

I don't even know if it would be courage, or plain foolishness. I can't seem to settle the matter in my mind. Courage isn't the only thing I can't reconcile in my head anymore.

Most days I think it is best to let everyone go on thinking I am dead. A lot of the time, I feel so numbed I might as well be. Just because a man is breathing don't make him alive.

I'd appreciate it if you wouldn't mention this letter to Maizee or Leela. I'd like you to keep it between the two of us for now. But if you aren't too put out, I'd appreciate it if you would write back and tell me how Rain is doing.

You can write to me care of The Cathedral of Notre-Dame, 4 Rue du Général de Dais, 14400 Bayeux, France. I know I owe you an explanation. Maybe one day, if I can ever get it sorted out enough in my own mind, I'll be able to explain it to you.

    Zeb

Turning the tissue-thin stationery over in her stubby fingers, Burdy dropped her head and did something rare—she wept.

Chapter 12

Two weeks passed before Burdy collected her thoughts enough to write Zeb back. Two very long weeks. She must've reread the letter a hundred times, pulling it out of her apron pocket every morning after breakfast, every night after dinner.

When that first Saturday came around, Burdy put on her boots and hiked up to the gravehouse in the meadow. In a poke, she carried a biscuit and fatback as an offering for Tibbis, her dead husband.

Burdy eased down beside the boulder that served as Tibbis's gravestone. She'd hauled the boulder down from Horseshoe Falls herself the first year after Tibbis died. She could carry it still, if need be. Burdy was every bit as strong at forty as she had been at twenty. Stronger maybe.

She noticed a smear of blood on her forearm. Likely a scratch from climbing up through the laurel slick. The pathway was nearly grown over since few folks besides her came up this side of the mountain anymore. If she'd thought about it ahead of time, she would have brought the swingblade, hacked a cleaner path.

Town work didn't leave folks much time for outdoor hiking. Not like they used to do. When Tibbis was around, he kept the path cleared. But during the war, a lot of folks from the Bend had taken jobs uptown at the munitions plant.

Besides, after that lunatic Tony Crow came down from the mountain last Easter, claiming God gave him a vision, and not a good one but one of damnation and destruction, there weren't too many folks keen to head up to the high meadows alone for fear God might meet them there. People at the Bend, and most folks in town, only liked meeting God inside the church building, where he could be contained. Or at least corralled a bit.

Before mentioning the letter from Zeb, Burdy got Tibbis all caught up on the regular news. She told him about how Mayne, the postmistress at Pressmen's home, had gone to work sick with an upset stomach one morning and got stuck in the bathroom.

"She had the runs so bad she had to excuse herself right in the middle of helping Mr. Puffin, who was mailing a package to his girl out in California.

"You remember little Mollie Matilda? She grew up to be a real beauty, won Miss Tennessee a few years back, remember I told you? She had her own daytime talk show in Nashville and everything. Then she married some TV producer and moved off to Hollywood. She's got a movie coming out next year.

"Mr. Puffin was telling Mayne all about the movie when a cramp hit Mayne so fierce she thought she might shit herself right there in front of God and everybody. So she just turned and ran for the bathroom. And wouldn't you know it, it was right when the lunchtime line was plumb out the door.

"Well, that post office is so small, Mayne is the only employee. Thankfully, she made it to the pot in time but—" Burdy interrupted her own self laughing, recalling the sounds Mayne made as she'd told the story. "She'd done her business before she realized that she was completely out of toilet tissue. There wasn't a speck of paper in that entire bathroom. Nothing. Not even a magazine she could wipe with.

"Mayne didn't have no choice. She sat on that pot hollering for somebody to come help her, until righteous Mrs. Tufts got out of her place in line and went to see what the hollering was about. Mayne was so humiliated. Of all people to stand on the other side of the door asking her what the matter, it had to be Mrs. Tufts. Lawsie." Burdy was laughing hard now.

41

"Well, don't you know Mrs. Tufts had her purse with her! I've suspected for a long time now that purse is nothing but a well-disguised growth. I bet she carries it to bed with her. Poor Mr. Tufts probably has a time cuddling up to her with that purse in the crook of her arm. Mayne got tickled when I told her that. But she told me she was thankful Mrs. Tufts had that purse with her because she had a package of Kleenexes in it. She slipped them under the door for Mayne. I told Mayne that's what she gets for going into work when she had the runs. I also told her that's what she gets for eating at Sisters Restaurant in Rogersville. That place is so nasty I can't imagine how Irva and Ina manage to stay in business. Neither one of those Collier girls ever learned a thing about hygiene or cleanliness. It's a wonder everybody who ever ate at Sisters hasn't shit themselves to death."

Tibbis didn't say anything. He just listened, like usual. Even in life, Tibbis never was one for swapping words. Burdy had long grown accustomed to his ways after all these years of marriage in life and in death.

She sat there in the stillness for a moment, listening as the wind hushed the earth. A green-feathered bird wrestled a cockleberry with its yellow beak. Burdy reached into her pocket and pulled out Tibbis's old harmonica. Then she began to play and sing "Sweet Fern." It was the song Tibbis had played the night Burdy gave birth to Wheedin. As she had labored in the back room, he'd sat out on the porch and played that tune. When he quit, Auntie Tay, who was assisting Burdy with the birthing, came out on the porch and told Tibbis to play some more.

"She likes it," Auntie Tay said. "It helps ease the work."

So Tibbis played it until Wheedin arrived squalling into the world. Then her daddy played it once more, matching her every squall with a yodel of his own. Such was Tibbis's welcome for his baby girl.

But when Burdy sang the words that afternoon at her husband's graveside, the song had none of its airish feel. It was dark and mournful, more desperate prayer than mountain ballad: *Oh tell me sweet fern, is he thinking of me? And the promise he made long ago? He said he'd return from over the sea. Oh why do the years go so slow?*

Tibbis was content to listen to Burdy, as it didn't really matter to him what she played and sang. He could have listened to her all day long and well into the night.

Burdy took out a blue kerchief and wiped the spit off the mouth organ, then folded them both back into her pocket. Tibbis had been too long gone to understand the significance of that song, but Burdy went ahead and blurted it all out anyway.

"I got a letter from Zeb the other day. He's in France." Burdy stretched out her legs and leaned against the boulder. She pulled her braid around where she could see it and began to unravel it. "He didn't have much to say. You'd think if he was going to up and disappear and let people think he was dead all these years, he might have plenty to tell in a letter, but he hardly wrote anything at all."

Burdy combed her fingers through her waist-length hair, careful to work out all the knots.

"I don't know what to make of it, Tibbis. I really don't. It makes no sense to me at all. Why would Zeb wait all these years to write? He had to know we was worried sick over him. Didn't he care about his boy? What would cause a fellow to up and desert his family like that? It ain't like Zeb."

As she sat there waiting for Tibbis to respond, a titmouse perched on the boulder, then hopped onto Burdy's shoulder.

"Pleasego. Pleasego. Pleasego," the titmouse hollered into her ear. Then that titmouse leaped up on the top of Burdy's head. Bracing itself against her scalp with its tail feathers, it began to tap in earnest, pulling at the wiry coils of hair framing Burdy's forehead.

"Maizee?" Burdy whispered. "Is that you?"

43

Chapter 13

She lied to everyone: Wheedin, Leela, Doc, Ida Mosely, Preacher Blount, Mayne, Dr. Jenkins, even Rain. Especially Rain. Some people don't think nothing at all about telling a lie. Auntie Tay said there is some that will piss on your leg and tell you it's raining. Those kinds of people often go on to build lucrative careers off the lies they tell, but Burdy was not the lying sort.

So while the lies didn't cause her to sit up late at night or fall to her knees at the altar on Sunday mornings, an uneasiness came over her and settled like a brick in her belly. She told herself that not telling the truth wasn't exactly lying, but she didn't believe it.

Tibbis had once sold twenty acres they had over in Goshen Valley to some distant cousin of his. Months passed before Tibbis fessed up to selling off the property, and then only because Burdy confronted him about it after she'd run into Ida Mosely at the library in Kingsport, who said she'd heard about the land sale from somebody else, though she couldn't remember who. Burdy figured Ida had been listening in to the party line again. Ida was bad to do that.

A person can dress deceit in fine silk, but a lie dressed in finery is still a lie. Even so, Burdy didn't tell anybody about the letter from France.

She'd written back to Zeb after the titmouse came and pecked on her head that day. Burdy wasn't sure whether it was Maizee's spirit visiting or not, but she figured she might as well not take any chances. It was one thing to have people upset with you. Quite another to annoy the souls of the dead and troubled.

Dear Zeb:

You couldn't have surprised me more if Tibbis himself had gotten up from his grave bed and come walking down the mountain.

Rain is doing good. He's in Knoxville, attending the School for the Deaf.

Everybody at the Bend is busy these days. Most people have taken jobs elsewhere. Doc is working at the munitions plant over in Mt. Carmel. I am working myself at a clinic uptown.

I see from your return address that you are at a church of some sort. Is it a church hospital? Is that why we haven't heard from you in all these years, Zeb? Will you be coming home soon?

Please write back.

Burdy

There was so much Burdy wanted to ask Zeb, but she knew enough from her work in the clinic not to ask too many questions right off. There was some reason Zeb had decided to write her when he did.

The Zeb she knew would not have kept his family in the dark for so long. He would never have abandoned his family, not for any reason. Burdy wasn't completely convinced that the letter wasn't a bad hoax of some sort, although her gut told her otherwise.

There was some reason Zeb had written to her instead of to his wife, although it was pretty clear he didn't know about Maizee. Burdy had already been a witness to what happens when disturbing news comes in the form of a telegram. She wasn't about to tell Zeb in a letter that his wife was dead and, even worse, that she had taken her own life.

Chapter 14

Zeb regretted it afterwards, dropping that letter in the mail. For years now, he had promised himself that he would never make contact with his family again. He'd told himself that it was best if they went on thinking he was dead.

And his death wasn't a lie. In most every way, the man they knew and loved was dead. He'd died on that battlefield next to Sergeant Harootunian, and he'd died a million times since then, in a million different ways, ways he'd never be able to explain to his wife, his son. Ways he couldn't even sort out in his own mind. He'd given up trying.

In the courtyard of Cathédrale Notre-Dame de Bayeux, Zeb sat hunched over, elbows to knees, cupping his left hand to catch the falling ashes from the cigarette he pinched between thumb and forefinger.

"*Bonjour le Sammy*," said Mrs. Arnoult as she walked past. Her black heels clicked soft against the stone pavement. A retired university professor, Mrs. Arnoult never missed the 7:15 a.m. Mass.

Zeb nodded, eyes downcast, watching as a merle picked its way around him in search of crumbs. From the tree above them, another merle sang. When he first came to Bayeux, Zeb liked the stuttered cluck-and-trill of these black robins, but over time, the noise had come to annoy the hell out of him. The least bit of cheerfulness pissed Zeb off. Whenever he found himself in the presence of anyone happy, he walked away, afraid of what might happen if he didn't.

He took another draw from the cigarette. He'd risen early that day, as he did most mornings, his hips stiff and aching, owing to the hardness of the mattress and the damage done to him.

Father Thom had made the arrangements for Zeb to come to Bayeux. He'd found him a place to live, two rooms on the back side of a bistro. Mr. Dupont, the owner, provided Zeb room and board in exchange for Zeb washing the crusted saucepans, filmy long-blades, slick broiler pans, ten-gallon stew kettle, and cobalt blue plates smeared with the orts of green beans, potatoes, rolls, butter, uneaten. It was mindless work and usually done when the kitchen wasn't so noisy. There was a certain solitude to it that Zeb appreciated. He didn't have to talk to anyone. He could just come in and do his work and leave.

Zeb preferred being alone. With the help of Father Thom, he had come to understand the language well enough to manage on his own if he had to, but Father Thom made sure he never did. He was the only person who referred to Zeb by his given name. Everyone else in Bayeux who noticed the veteran called him the same as Mrs. Arnoult—*le Sammy*—a term of affection derived from Uncle Sam.

The townspeople were indebted to the Americans for their help in liberating the city. Only a few miles inland from Arromanches, a small coastal community along the English Channel, Bayeux was the first sizable town to be freed. The locals fussed over Zeb as if he had slayed the German dragon singlehandedly. He hated that. He'd had nothing to do with liberating the village.

Zeb couldn't step outside without someone offering him a pack of cigarettes, a pint of fresh raspberries, a bottle of cider, or a cup of espresso. He kept his head bowed and dismissed all offers with a wave of his hand. He wasn't the one deserving of appreciation—those men were all dead. Zeb tried to explain that, but he finally gave up correcting the villagers.

He pinched off the lighted end of his smoke and put what remained in his shirt pocket. Unless he smoked it down to a stub, Zeb never tossed out a cigarette. Rising from the bench, he walked back to his apartment.

The one demand Father Thom made of Zeb was that he would never smoke inside. His routine was to get dressed, walk a couple of blocks over to the church courtyard, and smoke one cigarette before heading back to his apartment.

The twin bed was shoved up against the south wall. A wooden table with one rickety chair sat under a window that faced out across the back alley. The River Aura was just beyond the alley. That window and a kerosene lamp in the middle of the table provided the room's only light. Zeb pulled a scratchy Army blanket over the knotty cotton sheets.

An oak buffet table, scarred and splintered with age, was his kitchen. He washed what dishes he had in the white tin bowl that served as a sink. Two plates, one large and one small, were on a shelf under the sink. Four mismatched mugs, discards from a local potter, stood next to the plates. Zeb took out the green mug, the only one without a chip in the rim, and filled it with hot water from the spigot. He still couldn't get used to drinking his tea hot. He drank the warm water plain. Silver tea, Burdy used to call it.

Just beyond the kitchen area was the bath, the only other room. It wasn't much bigger than the outhouse behind Doc and Leela's place. There was a claw-foot tub, and a hole dug in the dirt floor that stayed eternally damp. Two marble strips ran alongside the hole, a place for Zeb to prop his feet as he stood or squatted to do his business. Stashed in the cupboard above the washbasin was a clear plastic tumbler, a water glass Zeb had borrowed from the bistro.

Each morning and each evening, Zeb reached for that tumbler. In the mornings, he removed his teeth from the glass and put them in his mouth. In the evenings, he brushed them and returned them to the glass. And each time he did, he remembered what he so desperately longed to forget: The gunfire. The metallic smell of smoke and blood mixed. The searing pain. The spiraling darkness.

Chapter 15

Burdy wrote Zeb, and he wrote her back, and she wrote him back, and they near about got to be pen pals. She hid his letters in the bottom dresser drawer, tied up with string and placed under an old flannel shirt of Tibbis's. She'd kept the shirt because it had been a favorite of his, and the fibers still held his scent. Even after all these years, that shirt gave off the smell of mown hay and river mud. Burdy would pull it out in the middle of a dark winter, hold it to her face, and remember those long-ago summer evenings sitting on the porch with Tibbis, watching a crescent moon rise up over a purple horizon.

She had never been with any man except for Tibbis, so she had nothing to compare the love-making to other than her own imaginations, but that was the very thing that kept her from taking up with any other man after him. Burdy could not imagine a better lover than Tibbis. She'd heard stories over the years from women friends. Heard tell how their men would come in from a day's work, and without even so much as a shower or a hand-washing, claw at their women's breasts, lift up aprons, push aside white-cotton panties, and drill them like a jackhammer.

The women who told Burdy these stories spoke in the same tone one might use to describe the annoyance of finding yet another roach under the sink. Having relations was bothersome, loathsome even, but it was something to be endured, part of every woman's life at the Bend.

Burdy knew that women who believed this—that men were simply that way and there was nothing they could do about it—did so because they lacked imagination. In fact, that was what caused them to settle for the wrong man to begin with. Had they expected better, demanded better of themselves and of the men they partnered up with, life might have gone differently for all of them. It certainly had for Burdy.

A woman has got to know herself well enough not to put up with meanness from any man. Burdy knew women who lived their entire lives and died troubling deaths without ever taking the time to know themselves. Women who were afraid of being alone with themselves. She never could understand why certain women feared being alone more than they feared being with somebody who mistreated them.

It was rumored that a woman over Clinch Mountain way had up and left her children, a whole gaggle of them, so she could chase after a singing career. Burdy didn't understand why a woman would want to leave Clinch Mountain for a city, any city, but she had to admit that if the rumor were true, that woman must have known something about herself that others couldn't see, couldn't understand.

The way Maizee did.

People at the Bend spoke often of Maizee, but never in daylight. They always waited until the skies closed their velvet curtains around the mountains before bringing up her name. It was like they needed the protection of darkness. They all feared that whatever evil spirit came had come upon her would descend upon them and cause their ruination as well. Burdy didn't share their fear, but she understood it.

The way Maizee's mind came unraveled was a terrifying thing to witness. But something about it all left Burdy wondering if perhaps Maizee hadn't known something that the rest of them were missing. Burdy was sure of this one thing: Maizee thought she was doing right by Rain when she did what she done. Maybe that momma over at Clinch Mountain knew it, too. Maybe she thought leaving her children was the rightest thing she could do by them.

Something about Zeb, about those letters of his, nagged at Burdy. On some level, she could accept that Maizee did what she had to do. Burdy didn't feel the same about Zeb. She didn't let on in her letters, but she was so angry at Zeb she could spit nails. If it hadn't been for him, Maizee wouldn't be dead. She'd be at the house, cooking up a mess of beans, or maybe in town working at the Holston ammunition plant. She might be working at Pressmen's, or maybe even getting her teaching degree over at East Tennessee State Teachers College in Johnson City. There was an endless list of possibilities about what Maizee could be doing right now, if only.

And how in God's green earth Zeb could abandon Rain the way he done, well, that was beyond Burdy. Rain adored his father, and up until those letters started arriving Burdy could have sworn on Tibbis's grave that nothing would ever have kept Zeb from Rain. Nothing but war, it seemed.

Tibbis used to say that even the best people could be hard to understand sometimes. Burdy had come to know the truth of that. Nothing about Zeb's disappearance and reappearance made any sense to her. The thought of him weighed heavily on her day in and day out.

She and Zeb exchanged several more letters before Burdy had the dream. She never asked Zeb too much about his life in Bayeux, and never revealed too much about life at the Bend. Zeb never asked anything about Maizee directly, and Burdy never offered up information. She didn't even say much about Rain, other than to tell Zeb about his schooling. He said he was pleased to hear that.

There's some that don't give credence to dreams, but Burdy wasn't one of them. Ever since she and Cousin Hota were young'uns, Burdy knew that her dreams were telling things. True, it had been her own momma who first told Burdy she had the seer's gift. And anybody with eyes that saw the dark-tinged handprint, the healer's mark, on Burdy's right side knew she was designed by Creator for his special purposes, purposes Burdy didn't always understand but trusted all the same. Ma Bay had predicted that Burdy would perform miracles. After the dream, Burdy became convinced that one of the miracles she was intended for involved bringing people back from the grave.

The night of that dream was an unusual night. She'd come in from Pressmen's worn flat out, and had decided she wasn't going to fix anything for dinner that required effort on her behalf. Instead, she grabbed a couple of cukes and some tomatoes from the garden and sliced them up on a plate, along with an onion that she also got from the garden. Then she poured salt into her cupped hand and sprinkled it generously over the top. Sitting at the table, her plate in front of her, she crumbled a piece of cornbread from Sunday dinner into a cold glass of buttermilk. Just as she brought a forkful of vegetables to her mouth, someone banged hard on the front door.

It startled her so, she nearly tripped over her own feet trying to answer it.

"Alright! Alright! Hold your horses!" Burdy yelled. "I'm a'coming." With that, she grabbed hold of the brass knob and yanked open the door. There on the other side of the screen stood Timmie Campbell, Little Fern's older brother.

"Mrs. Luttrell! Mrs.Luttrell! You gotta come quick, please," Timmie said. He was red-faced and sweating fierce.

Burdy pushed open the screen door. "C'mon on in, honey," she said, keeping calm just as she always did in the face of a crisis. It was one of the reasons people in the Bend turned to her whenever an emergency came up.

Timmie took hold of the screen door, but he didn't move from the porch. "I'm sorry to bother you at suppertime, Mrs. Luttrell, but it's Little Fern. Something's bad wrong."

"What kind of something?" Burdy asked. She reached into her apron pocket and pulled out a bandanna, handed it to Timmie. He took it and wiped his face.

"I don't rightly know. We was sitting at the table, eating supper, and all of a sudden she started coughing bad. Like something got stuck in her throat. Only she ain't eat nothing that could've gotten stuck."

"What was she eating?" Burdy asked.

"Mashed potatoes," Timmie said. "Momma made 'em. She's eat 'em before, but this time the coughing wouldn't stop, even after we pounded on her back. She's having a hard time breathing and her lips are all swoll up, so Momma sent me to get you."

"You run back home and tell your Momma I'll be right over," Burdy said. She turned from the door. "I need to grab something."

Burdy hurried to her pantry and pulled down the jars containing nettle and skullcap—the first for opening up Little Fern's airways, the second for settling her. From what Timmie said, Burdy reckoned Little Fern was having an allergic reaction.

By the time Burdy arrived at the Campbell home, Little Fern's momma was cradling her and pressing a bag of frozen raspberries against her swollen lips.

"Timmie, get me some warm water in a cup," Burdy said. She sat down beside Mrs. Campbell and saw she was doing her best not to cry, biting her bottom lip, her hands trembling. Burdy took the bag of raspberries from Mrs. Campbell. She saw the worry in this momma's gray eyes and the terror in Little Fern's brown ones.

"Everything's going to be alright," she assured them both. "You gonna be fine, Fern. It's an allergic reaction is all. I have some stuff that will fix you right up, okay." Burdy let Mrs. Campbell go on cradling the child as she took out the dry herbs and began fixing up a potion.

It wasn't long after Burdy gave Fern the potion that the child grew limp in her momma's arms and snored softly, the swelling in her lips subsiding. Her blond hair was matted with sweat, especially around her face. Her cheeks had the flush that comes with excitement, but that was to be expected. Even Timmie had flushed cheeks.

Fern's brother was sitting on the edge of the davenport, watching everything, ready to be of help if he could. Timmie was one of the good ones. Like most twelve-year-old boys at the Bend, he did as he was told and tried not to give his momma any grief. He might pick on Fern the way brothers do, but he loved his sister and it had scared him seeing her that way. Burdy reached over and patted his forearm.

"You done good today, Timmie. You were a big help. Thank you."

Timmie smiled. His heart was still thumping as he said a silent "Thank you, Lord."

Turning back to Mrs. Campbell, Burdy pointed to a red and swollen spot on the back of Fern's calf. "Looks like she got bit by something."

"Mercy," Mrs. Campbell said. "What in the world! I didn't notice nothing."

"Could be a bee sting, or wasp, or even chiggers," Burdy said. "Whatever it was that bit her, Fern had an allergic reaction to it."

"She's been bit by bees before and never had anything like this happen," Mrs. Campbell said, gently rubbing around the edges of the inflammation.

"These things can pop up anytime," Burdy said. "Somebody who has never been allergic to anything can all of a sudden develop a bad reaction to something they've been around all their lives. We don't know why this happens, but it can be very dangerous when it does."

Mrs. Campbell looked from her daughter back to Burdy. She nodded her head in understanding.

"You are gonna have to watch her good, especially when she's outside playing. Plant some mint up around the porch and along the edges of the yard. Mint will keep the bees and wasps away. Basil will, too. And make sure her teachers know about this." Burdy didn't want to alarm Mrs. Campbell, so she didn't tell her that such allergies could kill a child.

"I have never heard of such a thing," Mrs. Campbell said. "I am so sorry. I am so, so sorry."

"You don't have nothing to be sorry about," Burdy said. "It ain't your fault. You didn't do nothing wrong. There was no way you could have known. These things can just flare up."

"Thank you, Burdy," Mrs. Campbell said. Tears of relief washed down her cheeks.

Burdy put the herbs back in their respective mason jars. "Fern will probably sleep good tonight, but you come get me quick if she starts coughing or if it seems like she can't breathe."

Mrs. Campbell wiped away her tears and nodded. "Okay."

"Fern's going to be fine," Burdy said. "I know this like to have scared you to death. It would anyone. But don't worry about bothering me. Call me if you need me. Or send Timmie again."

Burdy's own heart was thumping more than usual, but she didn't let on. She knew she was just worn out. Whatever hunger she felt earlier was long gone. She simply wanted to go home and crawl under the covers. After excusing herself, she walked home, taking in the safe quiet that came with night in the Bend.

Chapter 16

At the house, Burdy wrapped her dinner and stuck it in the fridge. Then she dropped her clothes on the braided rug and slipped into a linen gown that Wheedin had bought her at some fancy store in Columbia. It was the softest linen Burdy had ever felt, and it fit her nice and loose the way she liked. It could be difficult to find anything that didn't fit snug over her large bosoms. Within minutes of laying her head on a feather pillow, Burdy was asleep and snoring loud enough to rattle the gates of heaven open.

And then the dream came. Maizee was on a train, Burdy sitting across from her. Maizee wore a bright yellow dress, not the blinding, harsh yellow worn by road workers but the soft yellow of newborn chicks. Her dark hair was cut short, and gentle curls framed her face. She was so pale, Burdy could almost see clean through her. But Maizee didn't look sick; her translucent skin give her the look of one of those models on the cover of a fashion magazine. Her head was turned toward the window, and she had a smile on her face.

Burdy was content to sit there and just stare at Maizee. But Maizee was supposed to be dead. How could she be dead and still sitting there across the way, looking more alive and the prettiest Burdy had ever seen her in this life? And why where they on a train? Where were they headed?

"How are the chickens?" Maizee asked.

"What?" Burdy said.

"The chickens. Do you still have the chickens? Gloria? Rock Rooster?"

"Raccoons got Gloria and some of the others. Rock Rooster tried to help, but he lost the battle with the coons, too."

Something dark flashed across Maizee's eyes. Her brow furrowed in what looked like consternation. Then she turned her head back toward the window and began singing softly:

"There's a place dear to me where I'm longing to be, with my friends at the old country church. There with mother we went and our Sundays we spent at the old country church."

Burdy tapped her foot and joined Maizee on the chorus:

"Precious years of memories, oh what joy they bring to me. How I long once more to be with my friends at the old country church."

They rode along in silence for a good while once the singing ended, Burdy watching Maizee, and Maizee watching the passing landscape. The view out the window was unfamiliar to Burdy, and the speed of the train unsettled her. She had never been in anything that traveled so fast.

"I got some more," Burdy said. She didn't wait for Maizee to respond. "More chickens. I couldn't let the coons be the victors. So I called up Cal Sloane and had him order me some. I have more chickens than anyone in the Bend. Forty-three at last count."

"Makes your name fitting," Maizee said.

"I suppose so," Burdy replied. She slipped Maizee a quick smile. It was good to know that death had not robbed Maizee of her sense of humor. Burdy worried that eternal life might be dull if heaven were off-limits to smart asses. She never told anyone, but Burdy often wondered if hell might have more interesting people.

"Is this the train to the tunnel of white light?" Burdy asked.

Maizee laughed so loud, her head flew back against the padded part of the seat. "Lord, no!" she said. "There isn't any tunnel of white light."

"There's not?" Burdy was genuinely surprised to hear that.

57

"No," Maizee said. "When you die there's no tunnel of light. There's only the darkest darkness. But it's not at all scary. There's a deep, deep peace that comes with dying."

"No River Jordan to cross over?" Burdy asked.

"Of course there's a River Jordan! That comes after the darkness. The Jordan is the wildest, scariest river I ever saw. And cold. Good Lord, that water is cold! Comes right down off the mountains. I thought I would freeze to death before I got acrost. I might have, too, if I wasn't dead already." There was not one note of irony or humor as Maizee spoke of crossing the River of Life. She recounted her story straight-faced, sober-minded. "I'll admit, I was shy climbing up naked out of that river onto the muddy creek bank on the other shore, even though weren't nobody around to see me."

"What? Your momma wasn't there? I thought for sure your momma would be there to welcome you to Gloryland."

"Oh, she come to find me in the pasture beyond the forest of lightning bugs."

"Forest of lightning bugs?"

"Yeah," Maizee said. She grabbed hold of the armrest as the train bore down on a hard left. Burdy realized that there was no one else on the train. No porter. Not one other soul. This concerned her, but she wasn't sure how she'd gotten on the train to begin with.

"When I come up that bank on the other side, there wasn't anybody there. I didn't know what I was supposed to do. Above me were the brightest stars I ever saw, but there was no moon to light my way and I couldn't see no more than a couple of feet in front of me. But I could hear singing, so I followed that sound."

"What were they singing?" Burdy asked.

"*Rank Stranger.*"

"I don't believe I know that one."

"No," Maizee said. "You wouldn't. It's a bluegrass song. It hasn't made it down to your neck of the woods yet, but it will."

"You'd think they'd be singing a hymn like 'Amazing Grace' or 'Rock of Ages,'" Burdy said.

"Oh, Burdy!" Maizee exclaimed, laughing. "The music is the best thing about being dead. It's like a living musical. There are jam sessions all over the place. Everybody can sing and play any instrument they want."

Well, one thing's for sure, Burdy thought, *being dead hasn't helped Maizee's mental state any. She still talks outta her head.*

"I headed toward the singing, which meant I was walking through a forest."

"Barefoot and naked?" Burdy asked.

"Yes, and shivering like a drunk in detox. But I'd only gone maybe twenty feet when I come upon a white robe hanging from the lowest branch of a tree. I think it was a hemlock. There was a pair of shoes sitting up against the trunk. Really nice shoes, too. Red ones made of the softest leather. I don't know who put them there, but they were a perfect fit. And that robe, it was terry cloth and so cushiony." Maizee wrapped her arms around her waist and hugged herself. She stretched her legs out straight as if she was slipping into those shoes again, grinning all the while.

Burdy laughed and said, "Oh, how I have missed you, Maizee. You and your crazy stories."

"I've missed you, too, Burdy. But it's been a glorious time, and I wouldn't give it up for anything. Anything at all."

"Not even the chance to be with Rain and Zeb?" Burdy asked.

Maizee froze. She pulled her feet back and sat up straight, holding on to the armrest again. She was no longer smiling.

"Soon as I slipped that robe on, all these lightning bugs began to flash together, at the same time. But they weren't in the trees. They were hovering along the ground. They looked like thousands of candles flickering, making a lighted path for me. I knew exactly where to go because the lightning bugs showed me the way.

"Momma was waiting for me on the back end of that forest. Daddy was there, too. He was crying like a big old bawl baby. Can you imagine that, Burdy? Daddy weeping over me. And Momma? Her eyes? They were back in their sockets where they belonged. The bluest of blues, staring right back at me. Oh, Burdy! It was joyous! I don't know how long we stood there, the three of us, hugging and crying and carrying on. It seemed like no time at all. A blink of the eye."

"It's good to see you so happy, Maizee," Burdy said, and she meant it. She wished nothing but happiness for Maizee, always had. While some in the Bend had bad-mouthed Maizee for her selfishness, leaving Rain motherless and fatherless, they knew better than to speak ill of Maizee Hurd around Burdy Luttrell. She had enough Melungeon blood left in her to rip their tongues straight out of their heads and feed it to her chickens if they ever spoke that way to her.

"Can I ask you something, Maizee?"

"Sure. Anything. You know that."

"Am I dead?"

"No."

"Then why are you here?"

"This is a dream, Burdy. One you need to remember."

"I doubt I could forget it if I tried."

"There's something I need you to do."

"What?" Burdy asked. She noticed her hands were sweating. She pulled a hanky out from her bosom, clutched it tight. Her knees were jittering up and down, so she crossed her legs.

"I know about Zebulon," Maizee said.

"I figured," Burdy said. "Given all this." Burdy nodded to the empty train.

"You need to go find him."

"What?"

"You have to go to France, Burdy."

"You really have gone barking-dog mad. I'm not going to France to chase down a man who didn't have the decency to come home from war! Didn't even try to make contact with his wife or child or any of us for years. Do I need to remind you that were it not for Zeb, you wouldn't be dead right now?"

Maizee leaned forward, placed her hand on Burdy's knees. "No, you don't need to remind me. There's a lot you don't know, despite your gifting. Zeb is not the reason I'm dead. I was sick, Burdy, very sick. Losing Zeb didn't make me that way. I was that way long before I met Zeb. Had it not been for him, I might never have had a chance at a good life. The best days of my short life were the ones I spent at the Bend with Zeb and Rain."

Burdy leaned forward, too, and put her forehead up against Maizee's. They huddled there, feeling the train's rumble beneath them and a holiness between them. Tears fell from Maizee's cheeks first, then from Burdy's.

"I'm sorry. I wouldn't hurt you for nothing in the world."

"I know," Maizee said. "I know. But I wouldn't ask you to do this if it weren't important."

"No, of course you wouldn't."

"Zeb's in a bad way, Burdy. He needs you, and I need you to do this thing for me. For Rain. Please."

"I'll go," Burdy said. She handed Maizee her hanky.

"Promise?" Maizee wiped her tears away and fingered the pink embroidered edges of the handkerchief.

"Yes, I promise," Burdy said.

Maizee jumped up from her seat, plopped down next to Burdy, and wrapped both arms around her. Then she slapped a kiss upside her head.

Burdy woke up to the cooing of mourning doves outside her bedroom window and a weariness in her bones that only the grieving know.

Chapter 17

Leela was down in her back for nearly a week after taking a spill in the garden. She had bent over to pick the last of the bush beans when she saw a white flash. She dropped those beans from her apron into her bucket. No time to mess around when there's a skunk in the garden, and him just three feet away from you. Leela didn't want to frighten the poor thing, so she stood still as a post, hoping it would just pass her by, leave her be. But that spotted skunk had seen her drop the beans.

When the skunk raised up on its forelegs into a handstand and spread open its hindquarters, Leela knew better than to stick around. She started backing out of the row fast as she could without further alarming the animal. She might have gotten cleared of it, too, had she not taken a fall over one of the tomato stakes she momentarily forgot was there. When she fell, the skunk dropped down on all fours and sprayed her good. The stench was bad enough, but the spray liked to have put her eyes out.

She'd taken to bed until the swelling went down in her eyes, but it turned out she'd wrenched her back something fierce, and laying in bed all day long only made it ache more. So she was sitting in one of the straight-back dining room chairs when Burdy came to the back door.

A month had passed since Maizee had appeared to Burdy in what was more a visitation than a dream. Afterwards, Burdy got busy preparing for the trip she promised Maizee she'd make. She told people she was going out West to Colorado to visit Cousin Hota. Most folks in the Bend didn't remember Burdy had a cousin Hota, much less remember that he lived in Colorado. But everybody was surprised that Burdy was taking a vacation. Long as they had known her, the furthest north Burdy had been was to Bristol, Virginia. Rumors of her leaving traveled through the Bend like blight through the chestnuts. Leela heard tell of it through Doc, who heard of it from Ida Mosely, who heard of it from the party line.

Burdy knocked on Leela's back screen door. She didn't wait for an answer, just knocked and stepped on in. That's how neighbors did one another in the Bend.

"I heard you took a bad spill," Burdy said. She placed a plate on the table. "I made you one of Aunt Bill's brown sugar pound cakes."

Leela put down the button box she was picking through and took off her glasses. "You sure know how to perk an old gal up. I love your Aunt Bill's cake." She pointed to a chair next to her. "Sit a spell."

"Mind if I fix me a drink first?"

"I'm sorry. I'd get up and get it for you, but I've wrenched my back. There's some tea in the icebox."

"Water will do," Burdy said. She dipped a glass full from a pail next to the sink and took a couple of gulps. "I heard about your encounter in the garden. I meant to get over Monday, but I've been so far behind I can't find my butt."

Leela laughed. "Burdy, you are a hot mess!"

"You are preaching the gospel now," Burdy said. She took a knife out of the drawer and a couple of plates from the cupboard. After cutting both of them a slice of pound cake, she finally sat down.

"How you been, other than the back?" she asked.

"Oh, doing okay. I always get outta sorts when I sense summer drawing to an end and the anniversary of my girl's death closing in."

Burdy let a bite of pound cake melt in her mouth. There was nothing to say that would cheer Leela when September came around. The month wasn't kind to Burdy, either. Best to just press on through it, the way one does when caught up in a frog-drowner. Put your head down and keep walking. Keep breathing. Learn to accept the drenching for what it is and try to find some beauty in it. That was what Auntie Tay had always told Burdy.

"What good would it do to rail against the heavens anyway?" Auntie Tay would say. "It rains on the just and unjust."

When she was a child, Burdy had no idea what Auntie Tay meant by such platitudes. But certain truths surface with age. Now, Burdy not only understood what Tay was saying all those years ago but sometimes even quoted those same words to the suffering men she tended at the TB clinic.

"I saw Doc uptown the other day," Burdy said, changing the subject. "He was meeting with the principal at Rogersville High about something."

"Yeah," Leela said. "We have that scholarship fund set up, and Principal Gipe needed to talk to Doc about it."

"You know if you need any money for it, I'd be happy to help out."

"No, it ain't nothing like that," Leela said. "We have it set up so that it will go on long after Doc and I are dead and gone. Just the gal who got the award this year wanted to meet us and thank us in person. But I cain't do nothing like that. So Doc went to meet with Principal Gipe and the gal."

"I saw the announcement in the paper about the scholarship," Burdy said. "I think Maizee would be really pleased that Kade's niece got the award."

"Yeah," Leela said. "I suppose she would be. I didn't like him coming around all the time when Zeb left, but I see things differently now. I know he was trying to help Maizee best way he knew how. I don't think he's ever got over her. But he's sure been a good friend to Rain all these years."

"Yes, he has been," Burdy agreed.

A gentle silence fell over the women as they finished eating their cake. They could hear children calling called to one another as they raced down the road past the house.

"There's a sound I don't hear enough of anymore," Leela said.

"Laughter?"

"Children. Not as many in the Bend as they used to be. People leaving, moving off uptown."

"Yeah. I hadn't really thought about it, but I suppose you're right. It does seem like a good bit of the younger families are moving off to Kingsport or Knoxville. Better-paying jobs. These young people don't want to work the farms the way their mommas and daddies did. Ida Mosely says her grandkids are averse to hard work. She figures her boys will sell the farm soon as she's gone. Those boys are both working up at Eastman plant in Kingsport. They got no intention of moving back to the Bend."

"Seems a shame for her and her old man to work all these years to hang on to that land, only to have her boys sell it off so they can buy a new fishing boat or whatever new toy they got a hankering for." Leela clucked her tongue like she did when calling the chickens to feed in the mornings.

Burdy picked up loose crumbs from the table with her finger and dusted them into her plate. "Leela, I was wondering about something the other day."

"About what?"

"You remember that doll that Maizee brung with her when she come upriver to live? That wooden one? I can't remember what she called it. Carried it with her everywhere, though."

"Yes. I remember," Leela said. "Why?"

"Do you still have it?"

"Yeah, I reckon so. It's probably in the attic with her other things. I know I took it from the house when she passed."

"I'd like to have it."

"What you want that old doll for, Burdy?"

"Oh, I don't know. Sentimental reasons, I suppose."

"Why Burdy Luttrell, I have never known you to be a sentimental woman!"

Burdy couldn't look at Leela for fear Leela might see something she didn't want to divulge, so she gathered up their plates and began washing them in the soapy water that filled the sink most of the day. "I don't know why you got to do me that way, Leela. You ain't the only one who loved Maizee. I loved her much as you."

"I know you did," Leela said. "She loved you, too. I'm sorry."

Her back to Leela, Burdy put the plates and forks in the drying rack and stood staring out the window. "I'm getting ready to go away for a bit," she said. "I'm taking a trip to Colorado. I'd like to take the doll along. I thought it might be a good charm to carry with me. That's all."

"What?" Leela said, pretending she'd never heard such a thing. "You're leaving the Bend? Whatever for?"

"I'm not leaving the Bend," Burdy said. "I'm merely taking a trip out West. Going to see my cousin Hota. I'll be back."

"I didn't even know you had a cousin in Colorado."

"There's lots about me people don't know."

"Now look who's speaking the gospel." Steadying herself on the table, palms down, Leela stood. "Come to think of it, I don't think that doll is in the attic. I think it's in the bedroom closet. I'm pretty sure of it." She groaned as she took her first couple of steps.

"You don't have to get it now," Burdy said, rushing to walk beside her, offering an arm.

"Might as well get it while it's on my mind and you're here," Leela said. She walked slowly into her bedroom. Burdy waited on the sitting room side of the doorway. She'd never been in Leela's bedroom before she tried to peer in without seeming nosy. A white chenille spread was pulled loosely across the iron-frame bed. A photo of Maizee from her wedding day sat atop the vanity, next to a silver-handled brush and a tortoise-shell hair clip. A shade was half drawn, and an oval braided rug covered the worn wood floor.

"Well, don't just stand there like a stump!" Leela said. "C'mon on over here and help me." She pulled the glass knobs on the chifforobe open. The smell of cedar filled the air. "It's back there. Push aside those clothes and them shoes," she instructed. "It's the shoe box on the bottom left. Yes, that one, the third one down."

Burdy did as she was told, reaching to the back of the wardrobe and slipping the box out from underneath the others. She handed it behind her, then closed the closet doors and turned just as Leela opened the lid.

"I haven't taken the doll outta here since I put it in," Leela said.

"When did you do that?" Burdy asked.

"The week we buried Maizee. She loved this old thing."

"Do you remember what she used to call it? I tried to think of its name, but I plumb forgot it. Hatty?"

"Hitty," Leela said.

"Yes! That was it!"

"I know that was it," Leela said. She handed the doll to Burdy and then lifted something else out from the box. A library book titled *Hitty*. Leela laughed. "Pretty easy for me to remember the name given Maizee left me this here little clue."

Burdy laughed too. "I had no idea there was a book that went along with the doll!"

"Yeah," Leela said. "Way I remember it, Maizee checked the book out of the school library the day she found Nan dead in the garden. Guess one of her little friends' brothers whittled the doll for her. Made one for his sister, too. Nan, Maizee's momma, sewed them matching dresses. When Doc and I picked Maizee up off the ferry that first night she come to live with us, she was clutching that doll like it was the last thread to Nan."

Burdy wiped the dust from the doll's face. The red nail-polish smile that Maizee and Eudie had painted on hadn't faded much despite the years.

"She's kind of a puny thing, ain't she?" Leela said. "That first Christmas Maizee was with us, Doc and I bought her a real pretty doll at Cal's shop. Thumbelina. She was a fat, soft plastic doll, but Maizee never loved her like she did this one. I told Doc she treated Hitty more like a sibling than a doll."

"Would you mind if I borrowed the book, too?" Burdy asked.

"Here," Leela said, handing it to Burdy.

"I'll bring them to you soon as I get back."

"When are you coming back?"

"I ain't quite sure yet."

"Is everything okay?" Leela narrowed her eyes, tried to assess why Burdy was acting so strange.

"Everything is fine," Burdy replied. She didn't want to get defensive, which would only make everyone nose around too much. Living at the Bend had its drawbacks. Everybody knew everybody else's business before sunset.

That night, over a meal of green beans, field peas and cornbread, Leela told Doc about Burdy's visit. "She wouldn't even say how long she was going to be gone," Leela said. "You don't think she's got a brain disease coming on, do you?"

"No," Doc said. He tore off a hunk of cornbread, ran it through the soup left by the peas, and shoved it in his mouth. "Unless you consider being independent a brain disease. Burdy Luttrell has always been a woman who did exactly what she wanted. She's not one for living her life to suit others."

"I suppose not," Leela said.

Before she went to bed that night, Leela got down on her knees on that braided rug, as she had most every night of her adult life, and asked God the Father to watch over her friend. She would repeat that prayer nightly the entire time Burdy was away.

Chapter 18

Burdy proudly made all her own travel arrangements. After visiting the library to read up on the different ocean liners making the crossing between New York City and France, she settled on the transatlantic steamer, the *SS United States*—or the "Big U." Once she saw news reports of actress Judy Garland taking a trip aboard the ship, she knew it was the one for her. If it kept Judy safe, it would keep her safe too.

She wrestled for a bit with whether she ought to buy a cabin ticket for $300 or a first class for $365. It wasn't like she couldn't afford it. She had lived frugally in the years following the unfortunate demise of Tibbis. He had left her land and money, and she'd invested thoughtfully. People in the Bend sometimes speculated on how much the Widow Luttrell was really worth. Some thought she had plenty, while others figured she lived government paycheck to government paycheck just like they did. Nobody knew for sure, and that was fine and dandy with Burdy.

She decided to travel first class. Some things just aren't worth cutting costs. Besides, Burdy had read in the newspaper where an Italian liner, the *Andrea Doria*, sank in the Atlantic somewhere up in the Boston Harbor. Dozens died. What was the point of saving money you'd never be able to spend? If she was going to sink, she wanted her last days to be memorable. She sent off a check for her ticket, taking care to post it at Rogersville so that folks in the Bend wouldn't be snooping all up in her business.

Before leaving the Bend, Burdy had called Wheedin and told her exactly what she told everybody else—she was going to Colorado to visit Cousin Hota. Like the others, Wheedin barely remembered that cousin, but she was delighted to see her momma go somewhere. Had Wheedin known her momma was going out of the country, she would have protested loud and long. But she never would have guessed it. In all the years she'd worked in Columbia, her momma had never even come for a visit. She hadn't felt the need to. Any visiting she and Wheedin did, they did in the Bend.

"That's great, Momma," Wheedin said when she heard the news. "It'll be good for you to see your cousin, to see the rest of the world."

"I hardly think Colorado is the rest of the world," Burdy replied.

"Maybe not," Wheedin said. "But it's a part of the world you haven't seen yet. You really should travel more, Momma."

Burdy hated when Wheedin talked down to her. She especially hated it when her daughter didn't have a clue what she was talking about.

Mayne dropped her off at the train station in Knoxville on the last Saturday in July. Burdy wouldn't even let her friend come in, just had her stop the car at the station's front doors, telling Mayne she'd be fine, she was a big gal after all. Mayne protested, but Burdy quickly thanked her and told her to go on with herself. Then she stood with her suitcases at her feet and waved Mayne off.

"Send me a postcard!" Mayne called out through the car window.

"Okay," Burdy said. She had no intentions of sending postcards to anyone, especially not to a postmistress. That would be like leaving breadcrumbs that led straight to Zebulon Hurd.

The train ride, Burdy's first, was pleasant. The smiling porter took her luggage and her ticket and welcomed her aboard. Burdy had paid for a private compartment because she feared all that chugging movement might make her sick. She needn't have worried. The pull-along motion had the same soothing effect of a rocking chair.

Burdy slipped out of the turquoise wool coat that Wheedin had given her several Christmases before. "It matches your eyes, Momma!" Wheedin had said, pleased at finding such a treasure at a little boutique during a daylong shopping excursion to Bristol, Virginia. And Burdy did love the coat, especially the way it matched her eyes and gave her skin a rosy hue. She hung it in the sleeper's closet and placed the yellow scarf from Leela around the hanger too. That had been a last-minute travel gift. "I hear it can get cold in Colorado," Leela had said. *And in France*, Burdy thought.

Settling into a cushy seat next to the private car's lone window, she dug out Maizee's library book from her purse. The doll, Hitty, was packed away in one of the two suitcases, shoved into the train's storage bins. Burdy wasn't quite sure why she brought them along, other than she thought Hitty might serve as a physical reminder of Maizee. Burdy wasn't sure if she would share them with Zeb or not. When it came to Zeb, there was a lot that she hadn't decided yet.

Zeb didn't know she was coming, for one thing. Burdy didn't want to tell him for fear he'd take off and she wouldn't hear from him ever again. She had an address from the letters they'd exchanged, and she knew the bistro where he worked was close to his residence. She had looked up the town of Bayeux on a map and booked a seat on the train from La Havre, where the Big U would dock, to Bayeux.

Opening the book, Burdy picked up reading where she'd left off.

"Oh, Hitty," Phoebe whispered. "I didn't think going to sea would be like this, did you?"

Burdy fell asleep somewhere between reading and watching the landscape blur by.

71

Chapter 19

Burdy woke aboard the train the next morning to hear the porter calling, "Breakfast is served!" Over a cup of steaming black coffee and too-crisp raisin toast, Burdy thought of her Auntie Tay and how odd it was that some long-ago conversation they shared had remained with her throughout her life.

Wild roses were blooming on the hillside by the house the afternoon when Auntie Tay first told the story of Rotherwood to young Burdy. Reverend F. A. Ross, a wealthy plantation owner, had the opulent Rotherwood mansion built in the 1800s on a bluff overlooking the Holston River. The view alone was worth millions. A person could see Bays Mountain and Chimney Top from the porches. There was a pool and a garden atop the roof of the two-story house built of gleaming white stucco, unusual for East Tennessee in 1819. Auntie Tay said slaves carried water from the well up to the top of the roof to fill the pool and to water the rooftop gardens. But that magnificent house burned to the ground. So the Reverend built him another, better home.

"Even more fancier than the first," Auntie Tay said.

Reverend Ross was the fellow who named Kingsport—King's Port. Auntie Tay said that part real slow so Burdy could hear it as two words instead of one. "But money don't buy you happiness," she insisted.

"Why do you say that?" Burdy had asked.

"Reverend Ross lost everything. His first home burned down. His daughter killed herself. Then he lost Rotherwood a second time when he was forced to sell it after he lost all his money in the cotton market. They say his daughter haints the house now."

"How come his daughter to kill herself, Auntie Tay?"

"She was the unluckiest of all women when it came to love."

Burdy tilted a pot upside down and dumped the old dirt over the fence before handing the pot to Auntie Tay, who filled it with fresh potting soil.

"Rowena Ross was beautiful," Tay continued. "She could sing and was smart as a whip. Her daddy paid for her to go off to some fancy school in New York or some other Yankee place I can't rightly recall now. Anyway, when she came back she got engaged, but the man drowned in the Holston right in front of her. Some folks say he drowned on their wedding day."

"Oh, that is awful!" Burdy said. She put her palms together and dusted the dirt from her hands.

"That ain't the half of it." Auntie Tay wiped the sweat from her face with the back of her forearm. "A few years later she got married to another fellow from Knoxville, and he up and died from the yellow fever."

"Did she have children?"

"Not then," Tay said.

"What do you mean?"

"She didn't have any children at that time, but she went on to marry once more and had a little girl. Theodosia Ross Temple."

"I don't think I'd want a name like that."

"Look at you, going around all puffed up like a peafowl. How is Burdy any better a name than Theodosia?"

Burdy didn't know how her name was any better. It just was, that's all, so she didn't answer. She patted the dirt around a newly planted tomato. "You still ain't told me how come she killed herself."

"I don't know if any of us knows why she did it," Tay said. "Maybe she never got over the loss of her first love. Maybe she was sad about the death of two great loves. There's some who think something happened to the little girl and that's how come. But that part ain't true. That little girl moved to Huntsville, Alabama, married, and had a family of her own."

"How did Miss Rowena do it?"

"Kill herself?" Tay asked.

Burdy nodded.

"I heard she walked into the Holston and drowned herself. Others say she hung herself inside Rotherwood. She can be seen walking along the Holston at night, carrying a lantern. Everybody around these parts calls her the Haint of the Holston now."

"I hope I don't never see her," Burdy said.

"I've seen her a few times."

"You have?"

"I have indeed."

"Were you scared?"

"Lord, no, Burdy. It's not the dead people you need to fear. It's the living. They's the ones that can really hurt you."

Auntie Tay's story, carried across the years, served as a warning to Burdy that this adventure of hers might bring her more pain. Love could often do people wrong, just like it had done to Miss Rowena.

Chapter 20

That bright August afternoon as Burdy approached the *SS United States* out of New York's Pier 86, she felt like another woman, a woman who didn't need to hide her diploma in a dresser drawer. And it turned out, none of the reading she'd done or the photos she'd seen prepared her for the moment when she first stared up at the giant embossed *SS United States* on the ship's hull. It was the most massive man-made thing she'd ever seen. Near as big as the mountains back home. Burdy felt a rush of patriotic pride as she tilted her head back to study the slanted red smokestacks. She felt a bit woozy, too. How could this mountain of steel not sink? Getting ready to board, Burdy felt afraid for the first time.

Not a penny had been spared in the building of this ship. She thought about the brochure she'd received after mailing off money for her ticket. "*S.S. United* is the fastest, safest, sleekest transatlantic liner ever," it said. She'd also read that the ship was designed by William Francis Gibbs, one of the partners in Gibbs & Cox, the company that designed seventy percent of the naval fleet employed during World War II. Gibbs was schooled as an attorney, but he hated lawyering. Burdy couldn't blame him for that. He took a different path and became a self-learned ship designer, the best of the best. That was respectable, Burdy thought.

The Big U carried 1,000 crew members and could accommodate 2,000 passengers. "It's like a floating city," Burdy whispered as she boarded. Nothing could compare to the glitter and chrome wonder of the *SS United States*. Burdy was sure of that, even if the luxury liner did smell a bit like the tractors Shug Mosely ran in his fields.

Dozens of handsome men in little white jackets, gray slacks, and black bow ties lined up to welcome the passengers onto the ship. A rain of red and blue ribbons fell from the upper decks. Burdy soon learned that some of these men were called "pursers," which seemed odd until she discovered that it was their job to see after the money exchanged. It was like having personal butlers everywhere she went, dozens of well-dressed men attending to the needs of hundreds of passengers.

During dinner her first night aboard, Burdy mentioned that the soup was delicious. And when the waiter came back with her dessert, he brought her an extra bowl of the soup. Burdy couldn't wait to get back home and tell Tibbis that she had eaten not one but two bowls of turtle soup! Her dining companions said they had seen the 200-pound turtle stroll aboard on the gangway.

"He was reporting for duty," the lieutenant said, laughing.

At first, she felt awkward about eating with strangers. When she arrived in the dining hall for supper that first night, she was embarrassed to discover the majority of the women wearing long gloves, satin gowns, and glittering necklaces.

She had no idea this was how a person should dress for a meal aboard a ship, although she at least had the good graces to wear her Sunday best, a pale blue dress made from a glazed calico that she had ordered special from Sears and Roebuck. The military men in their dress uniforms stood out even more against the backdrop of white linen tablecloths, fine china, and elegant red chairs. Burdy clutched her black handbag to her chest and looked around nervously. As she tried to fade into the drapes, one of the uniformed men walked up to Burdy and issued an invitation.

"Good evening. I am Lieutenant Colonel Jack Hoyt—Jack, if you will. My wife, Stacey, and I would like you to join us for supper," he said, offering his forearm. "Unless you are waiting on someone?"

Burdy was startled. "Your wife?"

"Yes," he said. "That pretty gal there with the rosy lips." A petite woman with a wide smile waved from three tables over. She looked like Grace Kelly.

Burdy thanked the officer and took his arm, allowing him to lead her to a chair. Over a meal of duck, garlic mashed potatoes, and asparagus—none of which Burdy had eaten before—she learned that the young couple had traveled broadly.

"We are on our way to our next assignment now," Stacey said.

"And where will that be?" Burdy asked. She stirred a sugar cube into a cup of black coffee. Drinking coffee at night bothered some, but not Burdy. She liked coffee after a good meal. Having it now felt comforting, like a little piece of home.

"Paris," Stacey said. "Jack will be working with USAEUR."

"What is that?" Burdy asked.

"It's an Army service command for troops we have on the ground in Europe," Jack explained.

"Have you ever been to Paris before?" Burdy asked.

"Jack has but I haven't," Stacey said. "I haven't always enjoyed the places we've had to live, but I have been absolutely giddy over this. I am so excited about the opportunity to live in a city so rich in history, art, and culture. Jack's last assignment was anything but that."

"Where was that at?" Burdy wondered.

"Fort Hood, Texas," Stacey rolled her wide brown eyes. "Between the heat, the bugs, and the dust, I feared I would shrivel up and die like a fig on a dry vine."

They all laughed.

Burdy liked Stacey Hoyt. Actually, she liked them both. They were courteous people willing to share their stories. She learned that Stacey had grown up in Pensacola, Florida, the daughter of a naval officer. Jack came from a prominent family in Mobile, Alabama. His father was a heart surgeon, his mother a distant relative to the Queen of England. The Hoyts had no children.

"It slays my mother. Absolutely slays her," Stacey said. "But Jack and I decided early on in our marriage that neither of us are interested in parenting. Kids need the stability of home and school. Jack and I love to travel, to take off at a moment's notice. You can't do that with babies in tow. Besides, I would be very upset if Jack was traveling all over the world and I was stuck in some piney-woods place with a brood of kids to tend."

Burdy loved being a mother and wished she could have had more children besides Wheedin. But she also wished all women who really didn't want to be mothers could be as honest about it as Stacey.

The waiter cleared their plates, asked if they would like anything else.

"I've never eaten so much in one sitting in my entire life," Burdy said. "I won't have to eat for a month of Sundays."

"Oh, but you will!" Jack said. "The dining on these ships is one of the best forms of entertainment."

"Well, if I keep eating like I did tonight, they'll be able to toss me overboard and use me as an anchor."

The three of them laughed together throughout the week. Burdy let the couple take her under their wings and show her the ropes.

"These are for hanging on to and maneuvering your way around the ship when we hit rough waters," Stacey explained one evening as they walked Burdy back to her cabin.

"Do you suppose we'll hit some bad weather?" Burdy asked. She hadn't given much thought to that possibility.

"We might," Jack said. "It can get a little dicey this time of year with the movement of cold winds coming in over warm waters."

"But don't you worry about it," Stacey assured her. "We are on one of the finest ships ever built. Everything will be just fine. You'll get your sea legs in no time at all."

Stacey Hoyt had a way of looking on the sunny side of things, and Burdy appreciated that in a person. She made up her mind right then and there that Stacey was a person she could confide in.

On a sunny afternoon, while the two of them sat on the deck, watching children in navy rompers pull on their mommas' white skirts and beg for this thing or that, she told Stacey the entire tragic story of Maizee.

"And that's why I'm headed to Bayeux," Burdy finished. "I need to know why Zeb didn't come home. The Zeb I know would never have abandoned his family like that. I need to know what's come over him."

She looked out at the deep, smooth water. The sun lit up a clear blue sky, the way it does in early autumn. Burdy and Stacey leaned back in their deck chairs and listened to the waters rumbling. Absentmindedly, Burdy fingered one of her braids and smoothed the green head scarf she'd tied on to keep the wind out of her ears. Then she patted down the corner of the plaid woolen blanket spread across her lap.

Stacey was silent for a moment as she mulled over Burdy's story. "Does this Zeb fellow know you are coming to see him?" she finally asked.

"No," Burdy said. "I feared if he knew, he might disappear again."

"And he doesn't know his wife is dead?"

"No."

"Will you tell him?"

"I don't know. I guess it all depends on the condition I find him in."

"And you haven't told his boy that his daddy is alive?"

"Oh, no!" Burdy said. "I could never do that to Rain. That poor boy has suffered enough. I couldn't get his hopes up about his father. What if Zeb has no intention of returning to Christian

Bend? Can you imagine how hurt Rain would be if he thought his daddy had willfully abandoned him?"

"Well, you will have to tell him at some point," Stacey said. "You can't let that child live his whole life thinking his daddy is a war hero when it's possible that he's more of a deserter."

Stacey's remark cut deep. Burdy had not allowed herself to consider the possibility that Zeb had turned his back on his country, as well as on his wife and child.

Chapter 21

Reluctant to get out of bed the next morning, Burdy marveled at the passage of time. She'd crossed the ocean in five short days aboard a ship! After experiencing a life of luxury for a week, Burdy definitely wished she had left the Bend sooner. But it was like Auntie Tay always said, "You can't know what you don't know until you know it."

They would dock at Le Havre by mid-afternoon, so she planned to join the Hoyts for a good-bye brunch at 10 a.m. She had a little under two hours to get showered, pack her things, and tidy up the cabin a bit.

Burdy didn't like leaving a mess for others to clean up. She'd always been taught that a person ought not to foul her own pen. Clearly, others on the ship weren't raised right like she was. Sometime after 1 a.m., she'd heard loud knocks and hollering just outside her door. Yanking it open, she found two giggling women. The tallest of the two doubled over and puked twice, right there at Burdy's feet.

"Can I help you?" Burdy had asked. She noted that some of the vomit had sprayed the bottom front of her nightgown, and some had settled between the tall women's bunched-up bosoms. The woman reached between her breasts, and scooped up a handful, and held it out, the liquid dripping between her fingers.

"Ewww," she said.

Burdy did not flinch.

"We were looking for Tony and Oscar," the shorter woman said, speaking with a Northeast Yankee accent. Her hair was the color and texture of straw, and she looked at Burdy with eyes rimmed in heavy black like a raccoon.

"I believe you have the wrong room," Burdy said. "Tony and Oscar's room is down two more doors." Giggling again, the women walked off.

Burdy knew where to send them because, all week long, women of various heights and breast sizes had knocked on her door looking for Tony and Oscar. After about the third time, Burdy had asked the cabin steward if he knew anything about the two fellows.

"Oh, yes, ma'am," the steward told her. "They are Hollywood producers. They have a suite two doors down."

"Hollywood producers, heh?" Burdy said. She huffed a bit as she said it, then clicked her tongue disapprovingly.

"Yes, ma'am," the steward said. "They are looking to cast for a new movie and are holding casting calls in their room."

"Uh-huh. I can imagine."

After the women left, Burdy looked at the mess they had made and felt bad about it. Still, there was no way she was cleaning it up. She settled for grabbing a towel from the bathroom and throwing it over the puddle outside her cabin door. Then she washed up, changed nightgowns, and went straight back to bed. By the time she awoke, she was looking forward to a cup of steaming coffee. She had half a mind to go pound on Tony and Oscar's door. She figured they probably didn't keep farmer's hours and wouldn't appreciate being woken before noon.

She pulled the covers up taut over the queen bed, moved her folded clothes from the dresser drawers, and took her suitcase from the closet. She put the suitcase on the bed and clicked open the lid. Then she felt around in the left-hand side pocket and pulled out a wad wrapped in several of her best linen hankies, tied off with rubber bands on each end. She grasped the wad between her palms as she knelt down by the bed and prayed.

"Precious Sweet Creator, you have made this world more wonderful than I ever imagined. Forgive me for my narrow-mindedness. Thank you for helping me to cross these wide waters

82

without a moment of seasickness. Thank you for granting calm waters, sunshiny days, and starry nights. Thank you for sending the Hoyts. Jack and Stacey are proof that good people can be found anywhere—even on a ship!

"Good Creator, you have delighted me my entire life. Why am I still surprised when you continue to do so? Please forgive me for those moments when I fail to trust you. Please take care of Leela and Doc. Watch over my Wheedin and hold her close. Be near Rain and help him do well in school. And, Father Creator, I would ask your mercies as I continue on this journey. I don't have any idea what kind of condition I might find Zeb in. Please steady my heart and direct my path. Grant me the right words to say, and help me know when not to speak at all. I'd ask that you give me listening ears, and a heart that is tender towards Zeb. Please help me not to judge. Give me understanding where there is disbelief. Help me to remember your stories and the many ways in which you held back your anger. You know it is difficult for me not to be mad at Zeb for deserting Maizee and Rain the way he done.

"Hold me back, Precious Creator. Hold me back. Do not let anger rise up and ruin me, or ruin Zeb. Grant us the sweetness of friendship returned. I have no earthly idea of how to help Zeb, or if he even wants any help. I'm trusting you to direct my steps and my words. Please send your angels to guide me. I don't mind telling you, Creator, that I am a mite feared of what lies ahead. Please send your angels before me to make straight my path. Not for my glory, Creator, but for yours.

"And for that boy we both love so much—Rain. Never for a moment let me forget that the purpose behind this journey is that precious, precious boy. I ask all these things in the name of your own beloved Son. Amen."

Burdy had rubbed the wad between her hands so furiously as she prayed that the rubber bands popped off. The gemstone, a translucent opal, came undone from its bed of white linens. Burdy cupped it in her right hand. It was large enough to cover her entire palm. The sacred stone appeared to be aflame, so Burdy quickly wrapped it back in the linens and packed it away. Every healer woman knows that where there is fire, there is danger.

Her great-grandfather's prayer stone had been passed down to Burdy. Her mother had given it to Burdy the night before she married Tibbis, with the warning that she was never to misuse the stone.

"A prayer stone is not to be used selfishly. Use it only for protection and help during life's most difficult times," her mother had said.

Burdy had heeded that advice and kept the prayer stone locked away in a jewelry box at home, rarely taking it out. The only two times she could recall having removed it from its keeping place were when she miscarried a boy at six months and again when she found Tibbis dead in the meadow. Both times, she had fallen asleep, crying, with the stone clutched to her chest. Grief was exhausting. The stone provided her with a strength and a hope that went beyond her.

Burdy was mindful that her prayer stone was infused with the power of all those who had gone on before her. Still, she believed that if there was ever a need for help from her ancestors, this trip was it.

Chapter 22

Burdy glanced at the clock on the dresser table. It was 8:45 a.m. She set aside a black skirt, white blouse, and purple jacket, along with her black pocketbook and black pumps. Unlike a lot of travelers, Burdy had the good sense to pack light. Whatever didn't fit in her suitcases or her pocketbook had stayed behind in the Bend. Hitty was small enough that she fit in the pocketbook, but Burdy packed her underneath a sweater in the suitcase to be on the safe side.

Burdy knew her hip-length hair wouldn't dry before the meal, but she decided to wash it anyway. That meant she'd have to wear her hair down, unbraided, something she rarely did. If she braided her hair damp, it wouldn't dry for days. Burdy was not vain about her looks, but she was definitely hair-proud. Her hair had been her glory her entire life. That's how come she never cut it off. She kept it trimmed so clean that the thick ends looked like the neatly stacked edge of notebook paper.

Her hair was a sun-streaked chestnut color, not black like Wheedin's. She smiled, remembering how Tibbis always wanted her to tie it back when they made love because he said it got in the way. He was serious about lovemaking, and seriously good at it.

As she stood under the warm shower spray, Burdy thought about snuggling in Tibbis's arms. It had been so long since she was with a man, Burdy wasn't sure she'd know what to do with one anymore. Did a body remember how to curl into another's after such a long span of aloneness? She turned her back toward the water, let it rain down over her as she took a bar of lavender-scented soap and lathered it over her skin. How Tibbis had loved her body—her skin, her hips, her breasts! He nuzzled himself against her every chance he got, including that last morning before he went off and got himself killed by that half-witted shitepoke kid from up at Johnson City.

"Aw, Lord, don't think about that now," Burdy told herself. She poured shampoo into her hand and began the work of washing her hair.

Burdy arrived for brunch fifteen minutes late. The Hoyts were already eating. Jack stood up and pulled out a chair for her.

"We thought you might have decided to sleep in," he said.

"I'm sorry," Burdy said. "I'm moving slower this morning than I should be."

"Your hair!" Stacey exclaimed. "I had no idea it was so long!"

Indeed, Burdy's hair was so long that she had to move it around to one side to avoid sitting on it.

"Oh, it's a mess this morning. I washed it and it's not quite dry enough to braid yet."

"It's beautiful!" Stacey said. "I've never seen anyone with such lovely hair. You ought to wear it down more often."

"You think so?" Burdy said, surprised.

"Yes, really! Most people can't wear their hair that long. It gets to looking like a horse's tail. But yours is, well, it's breathtaking, isn't it, Jack?"

Jack, who had his mouthful of waffle, nodded. Burdy laughed.

"Coffee, ma'am?" the waiter asked.

"Yes, please," Burdy replied. Glancing over the menu, she was stumped as usual by the multitude of choices: figs, peaches, chilled Spanish melon, calf's brain, broiled kippered herring, steamed finnan haddie in double cream, fried codfish cake, and every kind of pastry and jam imaginable. Burdy looked over at Stacy's plate and saw an omelet with mushrooms. Scanning the menu again, she suddenly felt ill. She was trying not to show it, but her nerves had the better of her. The thought of getting to Bayeux on her own and meeting up with Zeb was giving her a bellyache.

"I really don't feel too hungry this morning," Burdy said. "Some dry toast and apricot jam will suit me just fine."

"Yes, ma'am," the waiter said. "I'll be right back with your order."

"Thank you." Burdy placed the white linen napkin across her lap and pulled the cup of coffee closer.

"Stacey, tell Burdy about my friend I ran into," Jack said. He wiped the last bit of syrup across his plate with a final bite of waffle.

"Your friend?" Burdy asked.

"Oh, yes!" Stacey said. She spoke with excitement, the way she did about most everything. "I've been meaning to tell you but I keep forgetting! Jack ran into an old friend at the bar the other night after you went to bed. A real nice fellow. Anyway, he lives in Bayeux. He knows this Zeb fellow you are going to see."

"He does?" Stunned, Burdy set down her coffee and stared at Stacey.

"Yes, yes," Stacey said. "He said everyone in Bayeux knows your Zeb. Not too many Americans living there, he said. Anyway, he's going to Bayeux, and he's offered to escort you there. I hope you don't mind, but I told him I thought his offer was generous and wonderful. Jack and I have been so worried about leaving you today to go off on your own when you don't speak any French. I can't imagine how you would get by. So I accepted his offer on your behalf."

Burdy sat back into her chair as the waiter placed the toast and jam before her and refilled her coffee. A look of sheer fright crossed her face, and Stacey saw it.

"Oh, dear, I think I've gone and done the wrong thing," Stacey said.

Burdy reached across the table and patted Stacey's manicured hand. "No, it's alright, really. I appreciate your concerns. To be honest, I've been a little worried myself about how I was going to manage getting from Le Havre to Bayeux, and go about tracking down Zeb. It will be nice to have the help of someone who knows the town."

"Are you sure?" Jack asked. "Because I told Stacey that you are a woman used to doing things on your own. I'll be happy to let our friend know that you have made other arrangements. I'm sure his feelings won't be hurt at all."

"Oh, I'm so sorry, Burdy. I didn't mean to interfere. It's just that I adore you so. I hate the thought of you going off on your own. But Jack is right; it's really none of my business."

Burdy spread the golden jam over her toast and took a bite, then sipped her coffee. "I'll be fine, really. I don't want to be a burden to anyone, but if you two approve of this young fellow, I'm sure I'll be in good hands."

"He's not really all that young," Jack said.

"No?" Burdy asked.

"I think he's fiftyish."

"Yes, I think so," Stacey said.

"So does this fellow have a name?" Burdy asked.

"Oh, yes!" Stacey said, laughing. "I suppose it would help if we told you that before he joins us."

"Joins us?"

"Yes," Jack said. "I guess Stacey left that part out too." He turned and smiled at his wife, who looked embarrassed. "Clint Dumas. He's supposed to join us for a walk around the promenade in"—Jack looked at his watch—"fifteen minutes."

"I thought it would help if we all met together before you leave with him," Stacey added apologetically.

"Well, I reckon we ought to be heading that way, then, don't you?" Burdy said. She didn't bother finishing her toast, just gulped down the last bit of coffee and reapplied her lipstick while Jack helped Stacey into a red wool jacket. Burdy tried not to think about the butterflies in her stomach, but for some reason she felt like a schoolgirl heading off on a first date. A knowing came over her the way it did sometimes. All of a sudden like. Only this knowing told her nothing in particular. It was just a knowing that goodness awaited her.

Chapter 23

Clint Dumas leaned on the railing of the upper promenade deck, watching as a group of four women played shuffleboard. He wore gray pleated trousers, a white shirt, no tie, and a black, single-breasted jacket with peaked lapels. His dark hair was parted on the side and swept up in the front, a wayward curl falling onto his forehead. He wore a pair of black alligator-skin shoes. Thick, dark brows arched high above his gray eyes. He held a small, leather-bound notebook in one hand and a pen in the other, and every so often he would stop watching the women to write something in the notebook. He was writing, his head down, when the Hoyts approached him with Burdy lagging behind.

"You making a grocery list?" Jack asked.

Clint looked up at Jack and smiled. "*Bonjour*, Jack." His accent was clearly French.

"Well, it's closer to noon than morning. Sorry we are late."

"Not a problem. *Bonjour*, Stacey. How are you this morning?" Clint Dumas bowed his head and tipped an imaginary hat.

"I'm wonderful, Clint. A little sad about leaving this lovely liner behind today but eager to see Paris."

"*Oui, Mademoiselle. Belle Paris!* You're in for the treat of a lifetime. I have made some notes for you this morning of things you need to be sure and do while you are there," Clint said. He tore three pages from the notebook and handed them to Stacey. "I wrote down the phone number of Jean-Louis, an assistant of mine who lives in Paris. Feel free to call him if he would be of help at all."

"Oh, Clint! You are such a gentleman. Thank you!" Stacey said. She reached for Burdy, who was standing a step behind her, and yanked on her coat sleeve. "Didn't I tell you? See, he's such a gentleman."

"Yes, you did," Burdy replied in a voice that was braver than she felt. She stepped forward so that she stood directly beside Stacey.

"Clint, I want you to meet Mrs. Luttrell," Stacey said.

Clint took Burdy's offered hand, and, instead of shaking it, he bent at the waist and kissed the back of it. "*Bonjour*, Mrs. Luttrell," he said. "*Enchanté de vous.*" Then, giving Burdy a quick wink, he translated his greeting. "Enchanted to meet you."

"Burdy," she corrected, stiffening at this stranger's display of familiarity. Back home in the Bend, people often hugged as a way of greeting others, even those they rarely knew. But this was not the Bend, and Burdy was not the hugging type even at home. Never mind the kissing type.

"Birdie?" Clint asked. "Like the *Mésange Bleue* that call to me in my garden each morning?"

"Mess-what Blue?" Burdy said.

"*Mésange Bleue.* Blue tit bird," Clint said. "Please pardon my French."

"Ha!" Burdy said. "My name sounds the same, but it's spelled differently."

"How do you spell it?"

"B-U-R-D-Y."

"Aha. I see then. *Pardonnez-moi, s'il vous Plaît,*" Burdy. And please call me Clint." He smiled, a generous and natural expression. Burdy liked that in a fellow. She smiled, too, trying to ignore her two friends, who were exchanging winks.

"Stacey and Jack have told me that you are making your first trip to Bayeux," Clint said.

"Yes. This entire adventure is pretty much my first of any kind."

"Really? Why is that?"

"I guess I never felt the need to go anywhere other than home."

"And where is home?"

"In East Tennessee. Way back in a holler."

"What is this you speak of? This…hollow?."

"Holler," Burdy repeated. "That's Southern-speak for a way-back place."

"A way-back place?"

"Yes," she said. "Way back at the end of some windy roads." Burdy demonstrated an S-curve with her hand. "I'm sure you have some way-back places in France."

"*Oui, Oui,*" Clint said, nodding. "We have many way-back places."

"Is Bayeux one of those way-back places?" Burdy asked. She noticed that Jack and Stacey had wandered off towards the bow of the ship, where they were leaning on the railing along with other passengers. She could make out the approaching coastline of Le Havre in the not-too-far-off distance.

"No, not really," Clint said. "Bayeux is not, as you say, a holler. It is not a way-back place at all. Bayeux is an old city, and although not very big, it is very large in history."

"I would like to know more about that history."

"I will be happy to share all I know, providing you answer one question for me."

"Only one?" Burdy said.

"For now."

"What is the question?"

"Is that your real hair?"

"Well, I didn't scalp anyone for it, if that's what you're implying," Burdy said, laughing.

"I'm not implying anything other than you have the most beautiful hair I've ever seen on any woman."

"Thank you," Burdy said. She reached up and pushed her hair back away from her face. The wind coming off the water wasn't all that strong, but it was enough to blow her hair every which way. "I fear it's a mess today."

"Not at all," Clint said. "It is lovely. I very much enjoy it."

Blood rushed to Burdy's face. She wished the Hoyts were still nearby. "Lovely" wasn't a word she was used to hearing in regards to herself. Men in the Bend thought of Burdy more like a favorite horse or a good heifer. Reliable. Dependable. Burdy could be counted on for a lot of things: A good axe if they needed one. A jar of shine. A box of kindling. The best shuckberry jam around. A healing. And, every now and again, a knowing that she could pronounce over them. But they didn't regard Burdy as a woman to be desired or pursued. She wasn't "lovely."

"Stacey told me about your friend in Bayeux," Clint continued.

"Yes, yes. You know Zeb?"

"This Zeb? Does everyone in your part of the world have such odd names?" Clint said.

"Yes, most everyone I know," Burdy replied.

Clint laughed. He was teasing her now. Burdy liked a man with a sense of humor. It was one of the things she had loved most about Tibbis.

"I don't know your friend, but I know of him. Everyone in Bayeux knows of him."

"So you have seen him?"

"Oh, *oui, oui*, many times."

"How does he look?" Burdy asked, although she was afraid of the answer. She had pretty well convinced herself that Zeb had suffered some debilitating injury, and that's why he didn't return to the Bend, to Maizee and Rain. She fully expected to find him in a wheelchair, both legs amputated. Or perhaps he'd suffered some sort of disfigurement. She knew from his letters that he must have

93

one good writing arm and one good eye. But perhaps only one of each remained?

"Look?" Clint asked. "What do you mean by this? How does he look?"

"Does he look healthy?" Burdy replied.

"Why, sure," Clint said. "Healthy enough. I see him at the Dupont's Bistro when I eat there, and sometimes at Mass."

"Zeb goes to Mass?"

"*Oui.* I have seen him there. He may go more regularly than I do. I am not as good about going as I once was. But your friend and Father Thom are friends. I think it was Father Thom who first brought your friend to Bayeux."

Stacey began waving at them. "Burdy! Clint! You need to see this! Look!" She was pointing toward something just off the bow of the boat. A crowd had gathered.

Clint shrugged and offered Burdy his arm. "Shall we?"

Chapter 24

Dolphins. A whole pod of common dolphins were leading the Big U through the channel into Le Havre. Burdy stood next to Stacey, watching as the dolphins leaped over one another, playing leapfrog in the blue waters. Having spent most of her life in the mountains near the Holston River, Burdy viewed dolphins as mythical creatures, something from a world far removed from any she had ever known. Laughing with delight, she looked to Stacey and Jack and the other passengers, and to Clint, and she shivered with pleasure.

"Unbelievable," she whispered. "Thank you, Creator."

Clint leaned his head towards hers. "Pardon, were you saying something?"

"I was just marveling aloud," Burdy said.

Stacey looped her arm through Burdy's other arm and wrapped it around hers. "Isn't this the most remarkable sight you've ever seen?"

"Pretty darn close to it," Burdy said. In her mind, very little could replace the beauty of Horseshoe Falls in October when all the trees were aflame, but standing on the bow of the *SS United States* as dolphins escorted them across the channel was certain to be one of the most glorious moments of her life.

She knew as it was happening that she would never forget the warmth of the sun on her skin, the wind in her face, the laughter in her ears, the sight of those dolphins leaping out of the waters, or the flutter deep in her belly. She felt like a woman in love, a feeling she hadn't experienced in far too long. She'd almost given up hope that she would ever know the thrills of life again.

Some deaths have the power to change entire communities of people. Maizee's death was one of those. The Bend was never the same afterwards. The Holston lost its glimmer. The mountains didn't seem as firm. The wild roses and honeysuckle didn't smell as sweet. People kept to themselves more. Fear can do that to a place, to a people—rob them of their zest for life. Everybody who had known Maizee, which was pretty much every person in the Bend, went away from her funeral thinking that if sweet little Maizee Hurd could lose her mind to the point of taking her own life, it might could happen to them, too. Burdy had never considered herself fragile of mind or spirit until after Maizee's death. That particular death took something out of Burdy. She began to wonder if perhaps everybody she encountered wasn't just one tragedy away from lunacy. But not today. Today she basked in the glory of Creator's beauty.

"We need to get going," Jack said. "It won't be long now before we're in port."

As happy as she was in that moment, Burdy felt a twinge of sadness wash over her. "I'm going to miss having you two at my side," she said, patting Stacey's hand.

"Promise you will come see us in Paris before you head back to the States," Stacey urged.

Burdy was reluctant to make any such promise. "Much as I'd like to, I can't promise you that," she said. "I don't know what's going to happen once I get to Bayeux, once I see Zeb."

"Nonsense!" Clint said. "Of course, you must see Paris! You cannot be this close to the most wonderful city in the world and not see its sights. It would be a travesty. I will take you myself."

"Okay, then," Jack said, chuckling at Clint's boldness. "It's settled! When your business is wrapped up in Bayeux, Burdy, you'll both come to Paris and stay with us."

"Yes, and afterwards, I will bring you back to Le Havre for the return home," Clint said to Burdy.

It had been years since Burdy had a man making plans for her. She wasn't sure she liked it, but she was in no position to protest.

She needed Clint's help. Truth be known, for the moment she was relieved not to have to decide much of anything.

Chapter 25

It was difficult saying good-bye to the Hoyts. It would have been even harder without Clint's sensitive handling of the anxiety Burdy felt. He stood quietly aside as she and Stacey held hands and said their farewells.

"Burdy, honey, I don't want you worry. Clint is a good guy. Jack has known him for years. He will take good care of you. You know we would never, ever do anything to put you in harm's way."

"I know," Burdy said. "I trust you. I'm not worried."

"Well, then what's this?" Stacey reached up and rubbed a worry frown from Burdy's forehead.

"I have a lot of things on my mind."

"Of course you do," Stacey said, taking Burdy into her arms and wrapping her in a long hug. "That's why Jack and I are so glad to leave you in Clint's care."

"Burdy, please remember that war changes people deep down inside," Jack said. "War can scar a person in ways that aren't visible. It is good that your friend has reached out to you after all these years. Please be patient with him. He has likely done some hard things."

Burdy nodded. She could not speak for fear of the tears that would fall. Now that she was standing on French soil, the earth didn't feel so steady anymore. Everything felt catawampus.

Clint stepped up beside Burdy and lifted one of her suitcases, adding it to his armful of personal luggage. "I don't want to rush you, Jack, but you and Stacey should get on if you have any hope of missing the late afternoon traffic."

"Yes, yes, we should," Jack agreed.

Everyone exchanged a final round of hugs and called out promises to see one another soon in Paris. Burdy picked up her other suitcase and glanced back over her shoulder at the *SS United States*. Clint stopped mid-stride.

"Funny how quickly a place can feel like home when one is far from home, isn't it?" he remarked.

"If you had told me that such a thing could happen, I would never have believed you," Burdy said. "I never thought I could feel at home any place but the Bend."

"We may be creatures of comfort, but we make our own comfort when necessary. And speaking of home, I am eager to show you around my hometown." He put their baggage next to the trunk of a shiny champagne-colored Mercedes and pulled out his keys.

"This one's yours?" Burdy asked. She'd never ridden in such a fancy car.

"I certainly hope so," Clint said. "Otherwise, we may both have to take the bus to Bayeux." He unlocked the trunk and loaded Burdy's suitcase next to his. "Well, look at that! We might even have enough room left over for a dead body should we need it."

Burdy looked into the spacious trunk and then cut her eyes sideways at Clint's remark. Her look did not escape him.

"Pardon my bad humor," he said. "A by-product of my years in the Resistance."

"The Resistance?" Burdy asked.

"*Oui.* Secret armies gathering intelligence to assist our allies. Very dangerous work, spying on the Germans, intercepting their communications, and lying to them about it. Hitler despised us."

"Well," Burdy said, heaving her other bag into the empty space, "it'll have to be a small body."

"A small one, indeed." Smiling, Clint walked to the passenger side and held open the door for Burdy. He bowed low. "*Mademoiselle?*"

"Thank you," she said, pulling her hair to one side and sliding onto the seat. "But should I be concerned for my safety?"

"Hitler is dead, remember?" Clint said. "I assure you, you are completely safe with me." He whistled an unfamiliar tune as he walked around to the driver's side and climbed in.

"How long of a drive is it from here?" Burdy asked.

"Depends on how fast you drive."

"How fast do you drive?" Burdy wished she'd thought to ask that question before she agreed to get into the car with him.

"For you, dear lady, I will drive the speed limit," Clint replied. He turned the keys in the ignition, revved the engine, and laughed. "We will pull into town in time for dinner. You must join me. I know where all the good food is served."

Burdy sank back into the leather seat. She shut her eyes and tried to relax, but her stomach was all bunched up inside. She felt lightheaded. Burdy wondered what in Jehoshaphat's name she must've been thinking, leaving the Bend and coming all this way by her lonesome and hitching a ride with a man she didn't know.

Clint turned on the radio and began to hum along.

"That's a pretty tune," Burdy said, opening her eyes. "I wish I could understand what that lady is singing."

"Hold me close and hold me fast. The magic spell you cast. This is *la vie en rose*," Clint sang. "Edith Piaf's 'La Vie En Rose' "— "life through rose-colored hues," or "life in pink." Burdy found Clint's voice pleasing when he spoke, and even more so when he sang.

Oh, goodness. She quickly looked away, pretending to be interested in the passing boats and cars. Clint was much more forward than any man she'd ever encountered. *Probably one of those fellows who chases anything in a skirt.* Stacey had warned Burdy that French men were flirtatious.

"They can be regular horn dogs that way," she had said.

"Horn dogs?" Burdy asked.

"Yes. Horny for sex."

Burdy rolled down her window a little ways and took a deep breath. France smelled different than the Bend or any other place Burdy had been, though she hadn't been many places. It had an unfamiliar spice scent, as if Creator had seasoned the air with herbs picked from his garden.

Clint lowered the volume on the radio and made a right turn out of the docks onto one of Le Havre's main roads.

"Would you like a quick tour of Le Havre?" he asked.

Burdy did like his voice. "You speak English so very well for a Frenchman," she said.

"My mother was American, my father French," he explained.

"Where was your mother from?"

"New York," he said. "My mother was good friends with Consuelo Vanderbilt. She met my father at one of those parties Alva Vanderbilt was famous for hosting."

Burdy had no idea who Alva or Consuelo Vanderbilt were, or what parties they hosted, but she knew enough to recall that the Vanderbilts of New York were some of the richest people in America. Did that mean Clint was rich as well? Not that it mattered. Burdy had all the means she needed for the lifestyle she'd carved out for herself. Still, she couldn't help musing over it. He seemed like such a common fellow. Put him in a pair of dungarees and boots, give him a good horse, and she had a feeling he'd fit right in at the Bend.

"Look," Clint said. He pulled the car onto a side street and pointed at a structure under construction. Burdy thought it looked like a concrete lighthouse. "This city was destroyed during the war," he told her. "Nearly every building flattened by bombs. The port was crushed. They've been rebuilding ever since. And as you can see, they use a lot of concrete. That is St. Joseph's."

"That's a church?"

"*Oui*," Clint said. "A Catholic church. That tower? It's designed to serve as a beacon for the entire city, day or night. It's a memorial to the war dead."

Burdy inhaled deeply. War dead. Up until that letter arrived at her home a few months back, Burdy counted Zeb as one of them. Now she didn't know what to think. Maybe he wasn't a war hero. Maybe he'd deserted. Maybe he was a traitor to his country. Burdy wasn't sure which sickened her more, the thought of Zeb dead or the thought of Zeb as a deserter.

Chapter 26

Burdy snapped open her purse and removed the train ticket she had purchased for the trip to Bayeux. "Guess I won't be needing this anymore," she said. She was about to tear it in half when Clint stopped her.

"Don't!" he said, reaching for her hand. "You can get a refund for it at the station in Bayeux."

Burdy looked askance. "You sure?"

"Quite sure."

Clint did most of the talking between Le Havre and Bayeux, pointing out sites he thought might be of interest. Burdy asked a question here or there. Sometimes she offered a bit of information about herself, but never anything too personal. When Clint asked if she was married, Burdy said, "Not any longer." She didn't care how good-looking Clint was, she didn't need—or want—a man all up in her business. As little as she knew about him, she figured it was best to keep private things private.

Clint wanted to ask if Burdy had any children, but he decided to postpone the question. It was clear that this woman was an odd hen, but not in a bad way. More like a mythical creature. Her eyes were translucent, aqua pools backlit with fire. Her brown skin and dark hair appeared sprinkled in gold dust. Clint understood why people would stop and stare when Burdy passed by. Yes, she was short and squat, but her presence invoked a majestic awe that Clint considered uncommon among Westerners. He even found her name endearing. And her accent? He didn't care what she said as long as she talked. This mysterious woman from the hills of Tennessee was intriguing, and he wanted to know more about her.

"What about you?" Burdy asked. "Are you married?"

"No, never," he said. He slowed the Mercedes and moved into the empty oncoming lane, cutting a wide swath around a man on a red bike carrying a bunch of sunflowers strapped to his back.

"These roads are just like the roads back home," Burdy remarked.

"How's that?"

"Narrow, curvy, and no shoulders," Burdy said.

"*Oui, oui*," Clint agreed. "Most of our roads through this part of France are like this. Unless, of course, one is driving in Paris. Then it is the crazy cabbies one must watch out for."

"Do you get to Paris much?"

"Paris. New York. London. Work is my life, my wife, and my mistress."

"What kind of work do you do?" Burdy rolled her window back up. Her lips were wind-chapped from the ship and the sun, so she took a tube of lipstick from her purse and reapplied it.

"Financial matters mostly," Clint said. "Government contracts, advising, not very exciting work, I'm afraid."

"I'm familiar with some government contract work," Burdy said. "Back home we have the Holston Ammunition Plant, the Oak Ridge site—that's where they built that atomic bomb they dropped—and the Tennessee Valley Authority. They built the dams that flooded our towns, drowned our dead."

"Drowned your dead? How can you drown people who are already dead?"

"They didn't move the graves of our people, even though they knew the dams would bury certain towns, make it impossible for us to return to the graves of our loved ones."

"That's horrible," Clint said. "Rest assured, I don't deal in those kinds of government contracts."

"Good. I would have a difficult time being friends with anyone who did."

"Whoa!" Clint laughed. "You are a feisty one."

"Yes," Burdy said, nodding. "I'd just as soon cut your throat as argue with you."

"I hope you are kidding."

"Best not put me to the test. Remember, I could fit you in the trunk." Burdy smiled and patted Clint's thigh. She could hardly believe she was flirting with a man for the first time since Tibbis died, and she didn't feel one bit guilty about it. In fact, it felt so good she wished they could drive off into the sunset, cutting up, laughing, and carrying on like the young people they no longer were.

"He died."

Burdy blurted out the truth, just like that. One minute she was laughing. The next minute she was telling Clint the whole ugly story of how she had lost her husband when that crazy kid from Johnson City shot him with an arrow and left him in the meadow near Horseshoe Falls. She told him how she'd learned to do all the things a man does, and to do them better than a man in most cases, and how she raised up Wheedin all by her lonesome, and how her daughter never, not even to this day, had gotten over the death of her daddy.

And because he listened attentively, Burdy went on to tell Clint about growing up Melungeon, and how that title made her feel set apart from others when she was a child. She had felt less than, not as desired as the blonde-haired, blue-eyed white girls. She even told him about the healer's mark on her side, and how her momma always said it was like Jesus had touched her with his bloodied hand.

Finally, she told him about Maizee and Zeb, about how she had tried to take care of Maizee the way Zeb had asked her to, but then Maizee got sick after getting word that Zeb was killed in action. She was so sick, in fact, that she slit her own throat down on the riverbank of the Holston not too far from home.

105

By the time Burdy got to the part about Maizee killing herself, she was tearing up, her voice cracking. Clint pulled the car onto a dirt road that led to a stone church grayed by age and weather. He stopped next to the walled-off graveyard behind the church and turned off the engine.

"I am sorry I have upset you," he said. His forehead was creased with worry.

Burdy wiped her eyes and blew her nose with a handkerchief Clint had handed her. "It's not you," she said. "I don't know what I'm doing. Maybe I shouldn't have come. Maybe this was a bad idea. I am so confused. One minute I'm so angry with Zeb I could, I could... Oh, I don't know, I could beat him like a rug. And the next minute, I want to wrap him up in my arms and tell him everything is going to be okay, even though I know it will never be okay. It is never going to be okay for Rain. He has lost his everything, and even if Zeb were to come home, it wouldn't fix anything."

Clint knew some things about this Zeb fellow that he wasn't ready to tell Burdy. The townspeople had found it odd, too, that the American did not go home after the war. Some had asked Father Thom why he stayed. Did he not have a family to return to?

Father Thom was responsible for bringing the American from Sainte Mère Église to Bayeux in those early months after the end of the war. He had helped the soldier get an apartment and a job. He and the soldier were often seen walking around town together in the evenings. They always looked deep in thought, so few bothered them as they walked. Sometimes, the American could be seen at the church helping out, cleaning windows, repairing woodwork, whatever odd job needed doing. He was often at Mass but had few friends other than Father Thom.

Unsure of how to console an upset woman, Clint asked, "Would you like to take a walk with me? I have something I'd like to show you."

"Here?" Burdy asked, looking around.

"*Oui*. The graveyard is quite beautiful. I think it will be good for you to get some fresh air before we reach town. We are on the edge of Bayeux now."

"Alright then," Burdy said. She kept a firm grasp on Clint's handkerchief as she opened the car door.

Chapter 27

A sign was posted next to the rusted, wrought-iron entrance gate: *Tombes de Guerre du Commonwealth.*

"What does that say?" Burdy asked.

"War graves of the Commonwealth," Clint replied.

Burdy shot him a wary look as she walked through the gate he held open.

"Trust me," he said. "There is beauty here."

Rocks crunched beneath their feet as they walked past graves that dated back hundreds of years. A gentle breeze rustled through wide-branched trees. The wind carried the spicy smell that Burdy had first recognized in Le Havre. She looked around for a flowering bush, hoping to identify the exotic scent. But the only flowers were in a window box outside the caretaker's home. Golden mums.

Delicate lace curtains hung in the window behind thick steel bars. The scene depicted in the lace could have been lifted straight out of Christian Bend—a barn, horses, and bright sunshine appearing over the hills. But the steel bars were an unsettling reminder of the dangers war had posed to the people of this region not so long ago.

Just past the house stood an iron cross, tall as a fence post atop a slab of old concrete. An intricate ivy vine, carved by some artisan's skillful hands, wrapped around the cross. At its center was Mother Mary, her hands folded in prayer. The elaborate crucifix was crusted with rust, as if it had been dipped in blood and left outside to dry. Burdy stopped and tried to read the etching at the base of the concrete, but she couldn't make it out.

"It's beautiful," Burdy said.

"Just God keeping his promises," Clint said. He began to recite a passage of Scripture, word for word, the way Preacher Blount did in his sermons: "To grant to those who mourn in Zion, to give them a garland instead of ashes, the oil of gladness instead of mourning, the mantle of praise instead of a faint spirit; that they may be called oaks of righteousness, the planting of the Lord, that he may be glorified."

"From the book of Isaiah, chapter 61," Burdy noted.

"So you know this also?"

"I do. One of my favorites."

"Mine as well."

"Yes, I could understand why."

Burdy didn't let on, but she was rightly impressed that Clint could recite Scriptures like a guitar player singing his own song. Being able to quote poetry or share an appropriate word from Scriptures was a telling thing about a person. It said they were paying attention, and that they saw connections between this world and the one beyond. Burdy cut her eyes toward Clint, thinking of the many telling things she'd noticed about him already. She realized that she truly wanted to know more.

She joined him, and they recited the next verse together: "They shall build up the ancient ruins, they shall raise up the former devastations; they shall repair the ruined cities, the devastations of many generations."

Then they stood before the crusted crucifix behind the little church on the road to Bayeux and said nothing until Clint took Burdy's hand. She did not pull away. It had been years since any man had reached for her. There wasn't a fellow in the Bend brave enough to try to make a move on her, but this wasn't the Bend. *And I'm not just the Widow Luttrell here*, Burdy thought as she and Clint walked past rows and rows of ornately carved headstones.

One was carved to look like two logs hitched together into a cross. Further on, three massive stone crosses were so old with age

109

that the ground beneath them had given way until they were leaning one toward the other. This made Burdy think of the old hymn, "Leaning on the Everlasting Arms," so she began to hum it softly. Before long Clint was singing the words, soft as the breeze blowing.

In the center of the cemetery was a towering memorial to the dead of World War I. Several miniatures of the crucified Christ were affixed to the base of the memorial with barbwire. Burdy half-expected to hear the oxidized Christ figures cry out, *Father, why have you forsaken me?*

"This church and these tombstones are mostly carved from Caen stone," Clint said, "a limestone that is quarried locally. William the Conqueror used this stone when building his castle and abbeys here. It has been one of France's most lucrative exports since the tenth century. The Tower of London, the cathedrals of Canterbury, and Westminster Abbey were all constructed from Caen limestone. Even in your own New York City, St. Patrick's Cathedral was crafted from the stone of Caen."

"Well, I'll have you know that we have some pretty famous stone ourselves around the Bend," Burdy said. She gave Clint's hand a light squeeze, glad that he had not let go. "Tennessee marble is pulled from the hills of Hawkins County and sold all over the place. It's a limestone, too, like your Caen stone, although it doesn't look anything the same. People like our limestone because it polishes 'til it shines like marble. Pink is the most popular of Tennessee marble, and while it ain't been used in any London towers or French cathedrals far as I know, it was used to build Lincoln's Memorial in Washington, D.C., and New York's Grand Central Station. And the most loved of all stone animals, Patience and Fortitude, the lions outside New York City's Public Library, were carved from Tennessee's pink marble."

"Uncanny, all the things we have in common, isn't it?"

Smiling at his comment, she continued, "There's even a region in Tennessee named the Luttrell Belt where they dig out the marble."

"Luttrell? That's your last name, right?"

"Yes."

"So do you get revenue from that?"

"Clint, I am an independent woman in all ways, including my money. Let's leave it at that, alrighty?" Without thinking, Burdy dropped his hand. She quickly realized that she'd spoken more sharply than she'd intended. Chances were, Clint was not prying.

"Pardon me, I didn't mean anything by my inquiry," he said. Privately, he could see why she might be offended, given how little she knew of his own background. Perhaps she thought he was interested in her money. If only she knew how rich he was, she would understand the absurdity of that idea. But he kept quiet and cocked his head at her.

"Why are you smirking at me?" Burdy asked.

"I find you amusing."

"As amusing as a snake handler in the outhouse?"

Clint burst out laughing. "*Oui*. Although, I hope to never encounter one."

"I did once, when I was much younger," Burdy said. "My Auntie Tay didn't have an indoor toilet, only the outdoor one. Shortly after supper I excused myself and went outside. I'd just gotten situated when I looked over and seen a big ol' snake curled up atop the Sears Roebuck catalogue Auntie Tay kept there for sanitary reasons.

"I'll tell you what! I jumped down off that seat and ran out the door with my underwear still down around my ankles. I liked to have tripped face forward."

Burdy was laughing so hard at the memory that she leaned into Clint's shoulder. He reached over and brushed back the loose strands of hair falling into her face. Slowly, their laughter subsided,

111

replaced by shy glances of tenderness and unspoken longing. Clint kissed the top of Burdy's head. She breathed in the scent of him, old books bound in leather. If the caretaker hadn't come around the corner with clippers and a bucket, startling them, Clint might have pressed his lips to hers. Instead, he pulled away and said, "We should get going."

Burdy nodded. She had to admit to herself, though, that she didn't want to go anywhere that took her away from feeling desired again. Oh, how she had missed the attention of a caring man!

Chapter 28

They pulled into town shortly after dark, and Burdy declined to join Clint for supper.

"I'm worn slap out," she explained.

"Breakfast then?" Clint asked. "You must let me introduce you to my town." He did not want to say good night. Not this way. Not until he was sure he would be with her again, and soon.

Clint put Burdy's suitcase down between them as they studied their surroundings. The desk clerk of the Hotel Churchill was busy checking in another client in the small, charming lobby. A lighted cabinet held artifacts from World War II: money, a lighter, postcards, a soldier's wallet, a flag, military caps, packages of bandages. Nearby was a rack touting the local attractions and eateries.

Framed black-and-white photos from the war hung behind the lobby desk and lined the walls up the stairwell. There were numerous pictures of Winston Churchill, all bearing his trademark sourpuss pout. Built in 1850, the hotel had obviously been through some renovations.

Burdy admired the lobby's chandelier and its rose-embossed wallpaper. "That wallpaper looks similar to the one hanging in the funeral parlor in Rogersville," she said.

"Is that a good thing?" Clint asked.

"Makes it feel kind of homey," she replied.

"If you insist."

Burdy studied the photos, looking for a familiar face, until the clerk interrupted her.

"*Bonsoir, Madame, comment est-ce que je peux vous aider?*"

"*Bonsoir*, Theirry," Clint said, reading the old man's name tag. "*Parlez-vous anglais?*"

"*Oui*," Theirry replied. "Not good but good enough."

Clint stepped aside, allowing Burdy to converse with the clerk. "You are in good hands now. I will see you in the morning. Ten o'clock?"

"Yes. Ten is perfect. Thank you, Clint, for everything."

"*Bonne nuit.*"

Her room, on the second floor, faced a courtyard. There was no fireplace, but there was a bed big enough for three and an adjacent bathroom, well-lit. Burdy appreciated a well-lit room of any sort. She unpacked, placing her folded clothes in the bureau drawer and hanging dresses in the closet that smelled like her cedar wardrobe back home.

"It is quare how much at home I feel here," Burdy said aloud. "You wouldn't have thought a person could find anything to make them feel at home all the way across the ocean from Hawkins County."

She sat Hitty up in the windowsill. "That way you can keep watch over the comings and goings of all the peoples," Burdy told her as she smoothed the doll's feed sack skirt. "And it ought to be bright and sunny for you here come morning. Much more cheery a spot than the corner of that suitcase or dresser drawer, I bet."

The last item she removed from her suitcase was the sacred stone. She took the opal from its linen wrappings, and, holding it between her palms, she knelt beside her bed and prayed. "Thank you, Creator, for the safe journey. Thank you for Clint and his help. Now please continue to guide me. Do not let my feet stray from the path you have set before me. May all I do honor you. Amen." Then Burdy placed the stone on the table next to her bed, where it would protect her as she slept.

After a quick shower, Burdy rubbed lavender lotion over her body, giving her calloused hands and feet an extra heaping. She'd made the lotion herself from beeswax and lavender oil, a hand-me-down recipe of her great-grandmother's. Exhausted, Burdy put on her gown, crawled into bed, and fell into a satisfying sleep. She was in France, but she felt so content that she could have been at home.

Chapter 29

Burdy rose that morning at the first break of light through the window where Hitty sat. Like most folks from Christian Bend, she had never been a late sleeper. Their lifestyles had long depended on crops and care of the land, so nobody could afford to be anything but an early riser. Even though times were changing, waking early was still in Burdy's blood. Around 5:30 a.m., she slipped into a pair of pants, pulled on a shirt and a jacket, and decided to go exploring before the town got fully awake.

The night before, the hotel clerk had given Burdy detailed instructions about her keys. Whenever she left her room, she was to lock her door and hang the key below the brass plate number of the corresponding cubbyhole in the lobby. That way, the clerk could look up from his post and know whether a guest was out and about. This provided a measure of security that Burdy found comforting and charming. If something happened to her in this strange town, at least the hotel clerk would be watching for her to return.

As soon as she stepped out the door onto Rue Saint-Jean, Burdy was glad she had put on a jacket. There was a chill in the air. She zipped it closed and shoved her hands into the pockets. Looking the right, she saw a leashed beagle pulling an older man down the street. The dog had his nose to the ground and never looked up once. His snout guided him from street sign to lamppost to curbside, his owner in tow. The man tipped his hat as Burdy walked by.

"*Bonjour, Mademoiselle,*" he said.

"Bon-your," Burdy replied. She was embarrassed, knowing she had not quite gotten the word right. Clint had insisted that she must try and greet the French in their language. He had made her practice during the drive into Bayeux, but the letters that curled rhythmically off Clint's tongue tripped off hers.

She stopped in front of a store window. Hanging above the door was a sign that read *Boulangerie*. Burdy had no idea how to say it. The only word she knew even similar to it was baloney. Or maybe lingerie. But baloney lingerie made no sense to her. Still, a person didn't need to be able to read French to recognize a bakery.

Stacked in the window were rows and rows of what looked like MoonPies dunked in food coloring: pink, yellow, blue, green, white. Even purple ones. A hand-printed card read *Macarons*. Burdy was pretty sure that the English translation wasn't MoonPies. A freight truck rumbled down the street, stopping at a corner market. Overhead, Burdy heard birds carrying on. She looked up but couldn't see them. Vowing to try one of these *macarons* before she left France, she moved on down the sidewalk.

From nearly every corner she passed, and over most of the rooftops, Burdy could see the spires of the Bayeux Cathedral. So she turned and walked in the direction of the church. When she came around the bend of Rue de la Juridiction, the size of the church liked to have taken her breath away. It was bigger than twenty Hawkins County courthouses stacked side by side and on top of each other. Burdy couldn't bend her head back far enough to take it all in.

She felt discombobulated by the sheer size of it, but its beauty slayed her. She crossed the cobblestone street and sat on a bench directly across the way from the cathedral's front entrance, an arched wooden door painted barn red.

"Oh, my good Lord. Oh, my good Lord," she repeated as if reciting a childhood prayer. The towering spires, the layered archways, the circular stained glass, the stories etched right into the stone. Burdy couldn't wrap her mind around the building of such a place. She shook her head, marveling at the creativity of man. Man could be so destructive, so hateful at times, slaughtering entire

117

populations at will. In the face of great evil, like that of Hitler, who had brought so much sadness to the people of this beautiful place, it was easy to forget that man also possessed limitless powers of goodness and imagination.

Whenever Burdy encountered anything of great beauty, she felt an echoing, as if that thing were calling to her, reminding her of a sweetness deep within. She felt that way whenever she stood under the grandfather chestnut up on Horseshoe Ridge, or hiked through the mountains when the laurel was in full bloom. She had felt it the first time she and Tibbis made love, and the morning she gave birth to Wheedin. She had wept then, salty tears washing over the infant child who was flesh of her flesh, bone of her bone. She had never known so deep a connection to Creator. It was the surest moment of faith in her life, a time when Burdy knew for certain that she was made in Creator's image.

The morning sun warmed the cobblestones, and Burdy unzipped her jacket. She watched as merchants unlocked doors to their shops. The chimes of the church rang out as locals began gathering inside the cathedral, preparing for Mass. The town was waking. Burdy had never been inside a Catholic church. She had a hankering to go to Mass and see what the fuss was all about, to discover how it differed from the services at her mountain church. But she was intimidated by her outsider status, as a Pentecostal and as an American, and finally decided against it.

She headed back toward the hotel just as Zeb walked under the church's stone archway into the cavernous darkness beyond. This was the nearest they had been to each other since the day Zeb left the Bend headed to war. But other than the shiver that ran down her neck, Burdy had no inkling how close they had come to one another in that moment.

Chapter 30

Burdy and Clint ate breakfast at a café around the corner from the hotel. He dressed casually in dark slacks, a white shirt with the cuffs rolled back, black loafers, and a gray scarf. Burdy opted for a blush v-cut blouse over a brown skirt. She matched it with a pair of rockabilly red pumps that Stacey had persuaded her to buy from one of the boutiques aboard the ship.

"Every woman needs a beautiful pair of red shoes," Stacey had said.

"Why in the world would I need red shoes?" Burdy protested. "I don't have a thing I could wear them with."

"Sure you do. Red shoes are like black ones. They go with most everything."

Ever the skeptic when it came to the latest fashions, Burdy remained unconvinced, but she bought the shoes anyway because Stacey was so adamant. Besides, as Burdy admitted to no one but herself, the shoes were pretty darn cute. That morning at the café with Clint, she worried that between the v-cut top and the pumps, she might be overplaying her assets. But as long as she was in France, she figured she might as well. She didn't know anyone except Zeb, and he didn't know she was there yet. She didn't have Wheedin and all the folks from the Bend prying into her life every minute. Hellfire, even if she had wanted to date someone after Tibbis's death, she never could have done it at the Bend, not with the way the people get all up in everyone's business.

The breakfast crowd had thinned out by the time Clint and Burdy arrived. Burdy couldn't read a thing on the menu, so she had Clint do the ordering—espressos and *Chaussons aux Pommes*. When the order came and Burdy got a look at the pastries, she declared, "Apple turnovers!"

"*Oui*," Clint said. "You don't like them?"

"No, no—I mean, yes, I do like them. I love them." Burdy turned her fork sideways and cut into the flaky crust. "It's just so unexpected, how much this feels like home. So many things are similar, like these turnovers. But then there are things like that church." She nodded her head toward the Cathedral Bayeux. "I have never seen anything anywhere like it."

"The Cathedral Bayeux has a long and storied history," Clint said. He took a sip of his espresso, his apple turnover only half-eaten. Burdy was wondering if it would be rude for her to order another.

"Please tell me," she said. "I love a good story."

Clint pushed aside the pastry. "The cathedral was consecrated in 1077 by William the Conqueror. He made his half-brother Odo the bishop of Bayeux. Odo's mother was the mistress of William's father. As you might imagine, that's a very scandalous background for a bishop. But one's spiritual abilities are too often determined more by wealth and connections than one's heart. William came to change his mind about his half-brother. He had Odo arrested and imprisoned in 1082 for raising troops without royal permission. The two brothers had a complicated relationship from then on out."

"Sounds about par for the course," Burdy said. "I suspect family drama is common among people from all generations and all nations."

"*Oui*," Clint agreed. "Undoubtedly. But it is assumed that William commissioned the Bayeux Tapestry. Do you know of this?"

Burdy shook her head. "No, I've never heard of it."

Clint called for the waiter and asked for the check. "Well, that settles it. First on our agenda today is a visit to the Bishop's Palace to see the famed Tapestry. It is a must for every visitor to Bayeux."

Burdy did not protest. She wasn't in town to be a tourist, but there was no reason not to go with Clint. She enjoyed his company. Besides, she had not yet figured out how to approach Zeb. Should she just show up and knock on his door? What in the world would she say? "Hey, Zeb, I was in the neighborhood and thought I'd drop in for a visit." No. Maybe she should send a note by courier and let him know she was in town, staying at the Hotel Churchill, and invite him to join her for supper. Or perhaps she should find the place where he worked and show up there. She just didn't know.

As Clint escorted Burdy through Bayeux toward the Bishop's Palace near the church, he told her stories about the people he knew in town. As he talked, Burdy saw that Bayeux was not at all unlike Christian Bend. It seemed that Clint knew most of the locals. They would call out *"Bonjour"* as he passed. Every now and again, folks waved at him from across the street or gestured from inside their stores. Clint stopped to chat with each one.

"Do you know everyone in town?" Burdy asked after the fifth such stop along their walk.

"No, not really," Clint said. "But we are a tight-knit group here. We became even more so during the war. We had to. It was how we managed to survive. Did you know Bayeux was the first town during the Battle of Normandy to be liberated?"

"Do you suppose that's why Zeb has stayed here?"

"Who can say what compels a man who has been to war?" Clint shrugged. "There are likely many reasons why your friend has made the choices he's made. Give him time, and he might share those with you."

They crossed a bridge over a small channel of water that ran through the city. Burdy admired the flowerboxes filled with mums, purple and gold. A local artist had placed his paintings all along a stone wall that ran the length of the river. They finally saw the man himself, bald with a beer belly, sitting before an easel and working with his brush in hand.

"The River Aure," Clint said, nodding toward the dark waters edged in mosses and lily pads.

"Can I ask your advice about something?" Burdy asked as they walked along slowly, looking at the artwork.

"Of course," Clint replied. "Fair warning, though: I offer you no promises about how good my advice will be."

"No worries about that. I just need to think this through. Before I try to contact Zeb, I wonder if I ought to first contact the priest and visit with him. This Father Thom. What do you think?"

Clint stopped in front of a painting depicting horses running on a beach. "Harness racing is a popular sport here," he said. "The sulkies like to train their horses on the beaches."

"Which beach is this one?" Burdy asked, figuring he had to think on her question.

"Hard to be sure, but if I had to guess, I'd say it's likely Omaha. But it may be Vierville-sur-Mer. Shall I ask the artist?"

"No, don't bother," Burdy said. "He's working. Sometimes it is best to let one's mind imagine."

"*Oui*," Clint agreed. "It is difficult to imagine the horrors that took place on those beaches while looking at paintings like this one."

"Well, who wants to imagine the horrors of war anyway?"

Clint turned away from the painting and looked at her. "Some people can't help but see them. Your friend, he may be one whose imagination is harnessed to war. I think it would be a good thing for you to see Father Thom. He may be able to help you help your friend."

Chapter 31

Zeb kept Burdy's letters together, tied off with a bit of red ribbon he'd retrieved from the bistro garbage following some customer's celebration, a birthday likely. The letters were stacked according to dates, oldest on bottom, latest on top.

He was surprised that Burdy bothered to write him back. He'd betrayed his wife, his child, and, by some folks' standards, even his country. Whatever shred of manhood he once possessed got left behind in the battlefield at Sainte Mère Église. He was a sorry excuse for a soldier, father, husband, man. He'd told Father Thom that, repeatedly, over the years.

"I don't know why God allowed me to live while he let good men like Sergeant Harootunian die."

Again and again, Father Thom tried to tell Zeb that war isn't an either/or proposition. That God wasn't handing out lottery numbers—man had done that. Hitler's slaughter was not God's idea. Hiroshima was not God's answer to world peace. All the evil, all the killing, all the horror was conceived by man, not by God.

Zeb always listened when Father Thom spoke of God's goodness. He figured there was no use arguing with a priest. But he couldn't get beyond that bloody battlefield. Couldn't get beyond the evidence that if Sergeant Harootunian hadn't insisted on helping Zeb that day during the battle, he might have lived. He might have gone home to his wife, his boys.

The thought of those boys tore at Zeb most. They were only eight and ten when their daddy died. The oldest would have graduated high school by now. Harootunian had told him that his boy wanted to play for the Sooners when he grew up and went to college. Zeb wondered if the kid had done that, or if his father's death had sidelined him from his dreams.

Zeb refused to think about his own family. It wasn't a matter of not loving them; it was that he didn't feel he had any right to think about them. Why should he be able to go home and watch Rain grow up when Sarge's sons would never see their father again?

"I don't see how a loving God could allow for so much evil in this world," Zeb sometimes said to Father Thom.

"Is it God who is allowing for it, or man?" Father Thom would reply.

In Zeb's book, it was God. God had the ultimate power, didn't he? God could have stopped Hitler with a heart attack. So why didn't he? Zeb couldn't think about such questions for too long because they left him feeling crazy angry.

Instead, he smoked. Whenever he got to the point where he didn't want to think anymore, he headed outside for a smoke. He smoked a lot. Something about the nicotine took the edge off. Or maybe it was the rhythm of inhaling and exhaling that settled his nerves. He always had a smoke after reading Burdy's letters.

One afternoon following Mass, Zeb sat at the table, untied the ribbon, and shuffled through the letters, running his thumb over the "Rogersville" postmark. He tried to imagine Burdy sitting at her kitchen table writing those letters, or walking out to the mailbox and posting them. Burdy never mentioned Maizee at all. Zeb figured she knew that news of his wife and child would only upset him. She wrote about Rain, but sparingly. Zeb read through those parts of her letters quickly. He could not, would not allow himself to think of his son. It hurt too damn much.

He'd been drinking when he wrote that first letter to Burdy. He never should have done it. He wished to God he had left well enough alone. He knew the military had declared him missing in action, knew that everyone back in the Bend took him for dead. He was okay with that. He should have left things as they were.

Zeb retied the letters and returned them to the rucksack where he kept then, then grabbed his pack of smokes and went outside. He pulled out a tobacco stick and lit it. Pulling a piece of loose tobacco from his tongue, he flicked it into the River Aure. Zeb liked that the river was directly outside his apartment door. It was a good place to smoke, leaning against the waist-high stone wall and watching the river below.

The River Aure was nothing like the Holston. Zeb considered it more a wide stream than a river. Only fifty miles long, it flowed into the River Vire in Isigny-sur-Mer, and from there out into the English Channel. The Aure fueled a small cotton mill in town, so there was that. Besides, having the river run through town provided Zeb with a measure of peace, something he sorely needed. Zeb always felt most at home near water.

He hadn't seen a waterfall since he had last hiked up to Horseshoe Falls. His boss at the bistro, Mr. Dupont, told him about the waterfall at Étretat, near the town of Le Havre, but Zeb hadn't seen it for himself and probably never would. Dupont said that the waterfall ran off the cliffs into the channel waters, but the tide had to be right for a person to hike to them.

Zeb had promised Father Thom that he wouldn't drink, and usually he was pretty good at keeping that promise. But there were times when drinking was the only way he could silence the screams in his head.

He took a draw on his cigarette and exhaled slowly, blowing tiny smoke rings. He liked watching how the rings started out small and grew wider and wider until they completely vanished. Zeb wished he could float off into nothingness like that. Completely erase himself from anyone's memory. He'd certainly made a good go of it, at least until he wrote that letter to Burdy.

The strange thing was he didn't even remember writing it until he received a return letter from Burdy. Then it came back to him in hazy detail. He'd started drinking right before the anniversary of D-

Day. The town had been abuzz, planning numerous commemo-
ration events. The bistro's regulars would sit around the tables long
into the mornings, drinking coffee and talking about where they
were when the liberation happened.

For them it had been so fast. One day they were under a Nazi
regime, and the next they were not. Beautiful Bayeux, thankfully,
had not been destroyed by the Germans like so many other cities.
The Cathedral was completely intact, as was the city. German
forces were too busy trying to defend Caen to worry about
destroying Bayeux.

Though Bayeux hadn't endured the bombings suffered at Paris
and Caen, its people still knew the hardship of war, of living in fear
of the Nazis. So great was their fear that in the week following the
D-day invasion, when de Gaulle came to Bayeux declaring
liberation, many locals had a difficult time accepting freedom. The
German occupation of their country had gone on for so long that de
Gaulle himself had not stepped foot in France in nearly four years.

"*Bonjour, Le Sammy.*" A couple of teenage boys carrying books
walked past, on their way to school. They looked crisp in their gray
shirts with matching pullovers and red scarves.

"*Bonjour,*" Zeb replied. He mashed his cigarette out on the
stone wall and flicked the butt into the river, gritting his teeth.

He couldn't help it; he saw Rain in the face of every boy. It
was the admiration in their eyes that bothered Zeb most. They
regarded the American soldier as a hero. They'd heard the stories
from parents and grandparents about how the Americans and their
allies had destroyed Hitler and his evil forces. For those boys, Zeb
was the town mascot for liberation.

Zeb had not been in Bayeux when the Tricolors were hung
from the window boxes and on the doorposts in celebration. He had
no memory of President de Gaulle's speech or of the locals singing
an emotional "*La Marseillaise,*" their anthem. Zeb's memories of D-
Day were not a cause for celebration of any sort. June 6, 1944 had

not been a day of liberation for him. It was the day he became imprisoned by memories he longed to forget.

So he drank. And he wrote that letter to Burdy. He regretted all of it: the letter, the drinking, the memories. The memories most of all.

Chapter 32

Clint made arrangements for Burdy to visit with Father Thom. He told the priest about Burdy's connection to Zeb, and explained that Zeb's wife had taken her own life in the months after learning that her husband was missing in action and presumed dead.

"War is always a tragedy," Father Thom said, "but never more so than for the innocent people caught up in it, especially the children."

Clint was familiar with the teachings of the church on suicide. He could even quote the Catechism on the matter: "Everyone is responsible for his life before God who has given it to him. It is God who remains the sovereign Master of life. We are obliged to accept life gratefully and preserve it for his honor and the salvation of our souls. We are stewards, not owners, of the life God has entrusted to us. It is not ours to dispose of."

For this and other reasons, Clint was unsure of how Burdy's visit with Father Thom would go. She understood very little about the Catholic faith, although, as she told him, there were plenty of people in her own faith tradition who regarded suicide as an "unforgiveable sin."

On Thursday night, Clint invited Burdy to his cottage for a home-cooked meal of pasta in a white cream sauce. She hadn't had a home-cooked meal since leaving Christian Bend nine days earlier. He told her the name of the dish, but she didn't have an ear for French. She could have sworn he said something about mussels. It didn't matter. Whatever it was, it tasted delicious.

After they cleared away the dishes, Clint poured them each a glass of wine and led her to a glass-topped table on the terrace, where he sat across from Burdy. "Can I ask you something personal?" he said.

"You can ask me anything you like," Burdy said. "Now, as to whether I answer you or not, that will depend upon the question."

Long shadows from the setting sun reached across the courtyard and stopped just short of their table.

"You said something, I think it was when we were on the ship, but it may have been when we were at that World War I cemetery, about having a gift—an ability to know things," Clint began.

"Yes," Burdy replied.

"I would like to know more about this gift of yours."

"Would you like to see the healer's mark I was born with?"

Clint nodded.

Burdy stood, lifted up her sweater and the blouse underneath it, pulled down the waistband of her pants, and showed Clint the mark on her right side, the one her momma claimed looked as if God had grabbed her around the waist after dipping his hand in the blood of Christ.

"Would it offend you if I touched it?"

Nobody had ever asked Burdy that before, not even when she was a child growing up Melungeon.

"No," Burdy said. She walked toward Clint, and he placed his hand on her right side, completely covering the stained handprint with his own.

"What was it you called this?" he asked.

"A healer's mark," Burdy said. "That's what my momma called it. It's what everyone in the Bend calls it when an infant comes into the world marred."

"*Le guerisseur divin,*" Clint said.

Burdy tucked her chin, raised her eyebrows. "You calling me names now?"

"The great healer-seer," Clint said. "Just like Nostradamus."

"Nosester-who?"

"Nostradamus. Perhaps one of the most famous of all Frenchmen. He wrote *The Prophecies* in the 1500s, troubling predictions penned in poetic verse. Nostradamus denied he was a prophet, but many regard him as the most accurate of all prophets. He predicted the rise of Hitler: 'From the depths of the West of Europe, A young child will be born of poor people, He who by his tongue will seduce a great troop; His fame will increase towards the realm of the East.'

"He was also *un guérisseur*, like you, a healer," Clint said. "At university, Nostradamus studied apothecary. He wrote a couple of books about natural remedies and cures."

"This Nostradamus fellow sounds a lot smarter than me," Burdy said. "Most of what I know I learned from somebody else. My momma and Auntie Tay taught me a lot about the roots I use for healing. And I can't help that knowing thing. It just comes over me, like the urge to pray."

"I have urges," Clint said with a slight smile. He traced his fingers along the healer's mark, sending shivers up Burdy's arms and through her spine.

For all her knowing powers, Burdy didn't know what to do. She knew so little about Clint, other than he stirred in her a deep longing that had been dormant for years. Unsure of what to say, she smiled nervously.

Clint slipped his hands around her waist, his fingers still stroking her bare skin, then drew her in and kissed her gently, longingly. Burdy's mind raced, but her body began to yield.

Clint pulled back and looked into her face for a moment, checking for any sign of resistance. Seeing none—for she had none to give—he kissed her again.

Then he took her by the hand and led her into his bedroom. She did not protest when he sat on the bed with the gold embroidered silk spread and kicked off his leather loafers. Nor did she put up a fuss when he reached around and squeezed her backside, then pulled her down on the bed beside him. Clint's kisses had weakened her in all the right places, and Burdy joined him eagerly. She was quiet, shy, nearly quivering, but not the least bit unwilling. She wanted this moment for herself, and she would take it. In the Bend, she might be the Widow Lutrell, but in Clint's bedroom in Bayeux, Burdy was a woman set loose. She never could have predicted what coming to France would reawaken within her.

Chapter 33

Father Thom saw himself as Zeb's protector. The priest understood as well as anyone that the pain of war continues long after the bombing has stopped. For many, liberation had come on June 6, 1944, but for others, like Father Thom and Zeb, it was a daily struggle to forget the things they kept remembering.

Survivor's guilt is the intolerable, belligerent bastard child of war. No matter how many rosaries he repeated, no matter how many candles he lit, no matter how many prayers of repentance he prayed, Father Thom could not forgive himself for not being there to protect Ysabel, his sister, when the townspeople of Cherbourg came for her, shouting, "*Catin! Catin!* Whore! Whore!"

They dragged Ysabel, only eighteen years old, out into the streets and stripped her down to her underwear. Then they yanked the crucifix from around her neck and tossed it to the ground, crushing it underfoot. Men and women, children and teens, all law-abiding citizens of France, hurled awful slurs as the foreheads and breasts of Ysabel and a dozen other women were marked with black swastikas. Ysabel and the others were shoved to their knees before the jeering crowd as churchgoing men took clippers and sheared their heads.

This public *tonte* was meant to humiliate the women, to pay them back for what the French deemed were wartime offenses. The terrified women were viewed as traitors to France. Most of them were young girls, like Ysabel. Some had swapped sexual favors with the Germans in exchange for food. Some had foolishly allowed themselves to fall in love with the enemy soldiers occupying France. Some had given birth to babies fathered by the Germans.

Ysabel, compelled by the Scriptures that taught her to love her enemies, to be kind to those who treated her spitefully, had returned the German's hatred with uncommon gentleness, prayers for their lost souls, a word of kindness, an offering of hospitality. It was not the Germans who beat Ysabel and humiliated her, but her own neighbors, people who knew her and had witnessed her deep and abiding faith. They were former classmates and religious teachers who knew that Ysabel's very name meant devoted to God.

These neighbors had mocked Father Thom's sister as she was paraded, shorn and naked, through the streets of Cherbourg. Adults and children alike taunted the young women, remarking about how they now resembled concentration camp survivors. The shame was too much for sweet Ysabel. She could not bear the thought of facing the friends and neighbors who had betrayed her, pointing and laughing at her.

That night when she was allowed to return home, she retrieved a belt from Father Thom's boyhood bedroom. She went straight to her room and stepped out of her white underpants, the only shred of dignity she maintained while being degraded through the public square. Ysabel climbed upon a chair and attached Thom's belt to the closet rod, and then, fashioning a loop around her neck, she hurled herself off the chair. Her brother's belt broke her fall and her neck.

After learning of the public spectacle, one of the nuns at the local parish had gone in search of Ysabel. Sister Tilda later told Father Thom that she found his sister with her eyes wide open. Ysabel had not even bothered to wash the swastikas from her body or the tear streaks from her face.

That same day, a young man in the crowd had retrieved Ysabel's necklace. Cupping it in his hand, he noticed that the crown of thorns was smashed so violently that it had fallen down around the neck of the crucified Christ. Other than that and the broken chain, the necklace was intact. The man shoved it tight into his pocket and stood aside as the crowd rushed forward, chanting and mocking *les femmes tondues*, the shorn women.

He did not follow them. Instead, he turned and headed in the other direction. He walked and walked until he came to the public gardens at the foot of the mountain and Fort du Roule. It was a place he walked through most every day. The pristine and orderly gardens calmed him, and the constant trickle of water from the fountains soothed his searing soul. No matter how chaotic his mind became, the stillness of the gardens settled him. Something about the place reminded him of the man he had been once, of the man he would never be again.

He weaved his way through the clipped shrubbery until he came upon the statue of the painter Jean-François Millet. The towering sculpture included a bushy-faced bust of Millet along with the statue of a woman with a small child in her arms, reaching up and placing a bunch of wildflowers in tribute to the artist.

Millet was known for his realistic paintings of a rapidly disappearing rural life. But in this statue, the man with the necklace in his pocket saw something recognizable, something of himself. It was the same something he had seen when he first happened upon a photo depicting the last known painting of Millet's.

He had been at the library in Cherbourg, flipping through books, trying to learn as much about France and its people as his limited French would allow. In the stack of books he'd gathered was one about Millet. The book said Millet was a source of inspiration for Vincent Van Gogh. But what struck the man with the necklace in his pocket was not *The Gleaners*, one of Millet's most famous works, or any other number of his golden pastoral paintings, but rather the most violent of his work, *Hunting Birds at Night*.

The man read that this was the last of the Frenchman's paintings, finished in 1874, the year before his death. *Hunting* depicted a desperation not present in Millet's earlier work. The golden light for which the artist was noted seemed harsh in this painting. With clubs in hand and bright lights glaring and hundreds of birds overhead, peasants struck madly at the sky and clawed fiercely at the ground.

The man understood such desperation. The day of the women's humiliation, he recognized it in the face of the young girl whose necklace he had retrieved, and he remembered seeing it in the faces of the German soldiers who stood over him in the bloody battlefield as he raised his own gun and aimed it. And he saw it now as he looked into sculpted oxidized faces of the bronzed woman and child laying flowers under the bust of Millet.

That woman and child reminded him of Maizee and Rain. Surely they, too, placed bouquets of wildflowers upon the empty grave in tribute to the man he once was, the man who had died among the hedgerows at Sainte Mère Église.

Zeb pulled the necklace from his pocket. His plan was to place it at the base of the Millet bust. But as he walked around the statue with the mother and child reaching, he uttered a prayer for the young woman shorn like a sheep in front of a jeering crowd: "God, help me find this girl so I can return her necklace to her."

Two days later, while in the library again, Zeb saw the woman's photo on the front page of the local paper. He carried the paper to the help desk and asked the librarian to tell him in plain English what the story said. She explained how Sister Tilda had found the young woman, Ysabel Gomont, age eighteen, dead in her home, having hanged herself with her brother's belt. Her brother was Father Thom, a priest in Bayeux, a town east towards Paris, about an hour or so away. A private Mass was set for Friday at the Cathédrale Notre-Dame de Bayeux. That was all Zeb needed to know.

Chapter 34

Ysabel took her life in August 1944, a little over a month after the liberation. Father Thom spent many hours imploring God to answer for what had happened. "How could a people who suffered so much under the Nazis turn on their own that way?" he asked, kneeling and clasping his rosary. He hands were large, the hands of a man who has yanked carrots and potatoes from the dirt, which he had done as a young man in his father's fields. His usually broad shoulders, capable of carrying the burdens of others, slumped now in heaving grief. His premature grey hair fell across his brow as he wrestled in prayer. "Having borne the brunt of inhumanity themselves, how could they have done this to my sister? To those other women?" But his pleadings were met with silence from God, leading Father Thom to conclude that even God couldn't explain man's capacity for cruelty.

Ignoring the commonly held belief that those who take their own lives commit an unpardonable sin, Father Thom performed the Mass for his sister. The God he served would not deny a broken girl. Ysabel had led an exemplary life full devotion to God. Yes, Scriptures taught that one should not kill. It was the Fifth Commandment of the Law of Moses. But Father Thom believed that it was not Ysabel who did the killing; it was the crowd who scorned her.

Zeb made his way to Bayeux for the girl's Mass. Following the funeral, he gave Father Thom the necklace. Finding that the Father had spent time serving in New York and knew English well, Zeb told him what he had seen Ysabel endure that day. Over the long afternoon and into the early evening, he answered every one of Father Thom's difficult questions.

"She wept when the angry men took her clothes and her crucifix, but she never fought back," Zeb said. "When they pushed her to her knees, she looked like her head was bowed in prayer. She didn't so much as flinch when her hair was shaved off." He stopped when Father Thom put his hands to his face and wept.

"Are you sure you want to know more?" Zeb asked. "What difference does it make now that your sister is dead?"

"Yes, yes, please," Father Thom replied. "It is important that I know these things. I understand it won't bring her back. But the truth matters."

Zeb pulled a handkerchief from his pocket and handed it to the priest. Father Thom wiped his eyes and blew his nose as Zeb finished the story.

"She didn't look away from those who taunted her. She searched their faces, even as they painted swastikas on her body. She kept saying something over and over again. Maybe a prayer for those who tortured her?"

"Yes, yes. Maybe," Father Thom said, his voice thick with grief.

Now, a dozen years later, Burdy sat across from the priest in his office, listening as he told her how Zeb had made his way to Bayeux in August 1944 to deliver the necklace of Father Thom's dead sister.

"You understand why I am protective of Zebulon," the priest said.

"Yes, I do," Burdy said. "But I want you to know that I have not come all this way to bring harm to Zeb. I love him like a son. He was my neighbor. I cared for his wife and his deaf boy while he was away. All this time, I thought he was dead. I would have gone on believing that if Zeb himself hadn't sent me that letter in June."

Father Thom's hands were folded in his lap. His red-framed glasses rested on the bridge of his nose. On a gold chain about his neck, he wore the crucifix with the broken crown of thorns, the one Zeb had retrieved from the streets of Cherbourg. When Burdy pointed at it, he scooted his chair around the desk and leaning forward, to show it to her.

"A talisman, for the remembering," Burdy said, gently touching the crucifix. "Not that you could ever forget." They exchanged a knowing look.

"I am not sure how I can be of help to you." Father Thom said. He sat back in his chair and folded his hands in his lap again. His eyebrows, barely discernible, were arched in curiosity.

"I was hoping you might be able to help me understand why Zeb waited all these years to contact me. Do you know why he never went back to the Bend?"

"The Bend?" Father Thom asked.

"Christian Bend," Burdy replied. She uncrossed her legs and tucked them under her chair like a schoolgirl. Few things made Burdy nervous, but she was learning that talking to a priest ranked at the top of that short list. "Home. It's home to me. It used to be home to Zeb, until the war took him away."

"I am not at liberty to discuss anything a parishioner has shared with me in private," Father Thom said. "Zeb is a member of our parish now, but even if he weren't, I would not be able to tell you what I know. It is Zeb's story. How much, if any, he wants to share with you is his decision, not mine."

Burdy sighed and stood up.

"I fear I have offended you," Father Thom said, also standing.

"No," Burdy said. "You have not offended me, but if I'm ever going to do what I came here to do, I best be getting about it before I lose all my nerve."

"May I escort you out?" Father Thom asked. "I'd like to show you our beautiful cathedral."

"I'd like that," Burdy said.

Their heels clicked as they walked across the stone floor. Burdy twisted, turned, and threw her head back so much her neck ached. She had never been inside a church as beautiful as this one. The rising columns, the repeated arches in the ceiling, the sculpted angels, the wrought-iron gates, the stained-glass story windows— everything about the cathedral was soaring. Majestic. Unimaginable.

"Do you know of Thérèse of Lisieux?" Father Thom asked. He had paused in front of a black-and-white photo of a young woman. Votive candles stacked in rows burned nearby.

"No, I don't."

"The Little Flower," he said. "She is one of the most popular of all the saints. She became at nun at the age of fifteen and died of tuberculosis at twenty-four."

Burdy thought of Maizee. It made her angry to think of folks dying so young. She felt a burn in her chest and blinked back hot tears.

"A simple girl, she never sought to be recognized. She only sought to serve God. She was tenderhearted towards all people. It was her tenderness, I think, that made her a writer. She wrote plays and poems but is best known for essays about her own faith journey. *The Story of a Soul*, her spiritual diary, was published the year after she died."

Father Thom turned away from the photo and looked at Burdy. "You might want to read it sometime. There is a quote of hers that I think is fitting for you. Something to keep in mind upon your visit with Zeb."

"And what quote do you find so fitting?" Burdy asked.

"*We should not say improbable things, or things we do not know. We must see their real, and not their imagined lives,*" Father Thom said. "Whatever imaginations you and others have clung to about Zeb, about his death, or even his service—whatever imaginations you may be harboring now—they may not in any way reflect the truth of Zeb and his experiences. Before you ask Zeb the truth, make sure you are ready to hear it." Father Thom pushed his glasses up and straightened the crucifix around his neck.

"And how do I do that?" Burdy asked. "How do I go about making sure I'm ready to hear the truth of what he has to say?"

"Pray," Father Thom said. "Pray a lot."

Chapter 35

After she left Father Thom, Burdy joined Clint for dinner. They ate at a restaurant bordering the river walk. The yellow glow from the restaurant's lighting reflected in the water. Clint didn't press her about her meeting with the priest, but Burdy told him the whole story anyway, even the details about Ysabel.

He listened carefully but thought it wise to say as little as possible. Burdy needed to be heard, and Clint intended to be the person who would hear her. Besides, what was there to say? "I'm sorry" didn't begin to convey the depths of his emotions about what had happened to those young women. And who could know what else this Zeb fellow had witnessed?

Burdy held up her glass of 1929 Romanée-Conti. "Wish me luck," she said. "I am going to meet with Zeb tomorrow."

Clint tapped his glass to hers. "I wish you the best of luck, always." He reached over and patted her hand. "God will be with you. Everything will be okay."

"I hope you're right," Burdy said. She took a long sip of wine. "I don't think I'll pop in on Zeb. I think I'll send him a note first, let him know I'm in town and want to meet with him."

"That would be best," Clint said. "It will give him time to choose his response." He finished his drink and poured more from the bottle that stood between them. "There is something I have been meaning to ask you."

"Yes?" Burdy took a bite of her entrée, roast loin of pork with chorizo and red wine sauce.

"I know you leave on Tuesday. I want to show you Paris before you go."

"I'm counting on it," Burdy said. "We promised Stacey and Jack."

"We did, didn't we?" Burdy saw a hint of sadness in his smile, but she couldn't think on that now.

Before she sent Zeb a note, Burdy did as the priest told her—she prayed. She'd been praying all along, of course, but Thursday night, following her dinner with Clint, she prayed with a bold intensity. Unable to sleep, she actually spent most of the evening and into the early morning in prayer. She prayed so much that her great-grandfather's prayer stone, which she grasped between her hands, glowed like fire in the dark of night.

Burdy prayed to God, to her mother, to Auntie Tay. She prayed to the Blessed Mary, to Maizee, and to her Melungeon ancestors. She called upon all the spirits of heaven to give her the right words to say to Zeb and the strength to say them. Finally, exhaustion overtook her. Burdy fell into bed shortly before daybreak, still fully clothed from her dinner out. She rose just before 7:00 on Friday morning. Then she sent a simple note to Zeb via a hotel courier.

The note reached Zeb during morning rush hour. He was helping in the kitchen because one of the cooks had gotten in a fight with the wait staff and quit the day before. Mr. Dupont called him in at 5 a.m. and put him to work, making coffee and croissants.

Zeb was not surprised to get the note. He knew Burdy was in town. There weren't many women in Bayeux with hair as long as Burdy's. He thought he'd seen her as he headed to Mass earlier in the week, but he'd only glimpsed her from the back, so he couldn't be sure. But last night, when he and Father Thom took their usual walk along the river parkway, Father Thom had told Zeb that a strange-looking American woman had come asking for information about him. Zeb knew right away that it was Burdy Luttrell.

"I should have known better," Zeb said.

"Known better than what?" the priest asked.

"Remember back in June, when I had that bout of a drinking problem?"

"Yes."

"I sent Burdy a letter. At the time, I didn't even remember writing it."

"June was a bad month for you."

"It always is," Zeb said. He sidestepped a dog pile that someone had failed to clean up.

"Don't worry," Father Thom said. "I didn't tell her."

"I wasn't worried. What does it matter if you tell her or I tell her? If I know Burdy Luttrell, she isn't leaving here without the truth."

"Yes, but how much of the truth you want her to know is yours to tell—not mine." Father Thom nodded at a mother pushing an infant in a pram.

"*Bonjour*," he said.

"*Bonjour*," she replied.

Zeb said nothing, just flicked his cigarette to the street and ground out the embers with the toe of his shoe.

"Did Burdy mention Maizee? My boy, Rain?" he finally asked.

"She did," Father Thom said. Upon learning about Ysabel, Burdy had told him the troubling tale of Maizee taking her own life. Father Thom knew that would be a hard, hard thing for Zeb to hear. His guilt would be overwhelming. But then, Zeb had been struggling with all manner of guilt for years now.

The priest told Zeb where Burdy was staying, but Zeb didn't contact her. Burdy came all this way to see him. He knew she wouldn't leave without finishing what she came to do. He simply needed to figure out what he should tell her. He was still thinking about it when the courier brought over Burdy's note Friday morning.

He sent a reply back:

Burdy,

I heard you were in town. Father Thom told me. I'd like to meet you at the American Cemetery at Normandy. It's only about 20 km up the road. There is a pine tree surrounded by rosebushes on the east side of the cemetery, nearest the overlook to Omaha Beach. I'll be waiting under the tree at 4 p.m.

Love, Zeb

Zeb told his boss that he would call someone else to fill the evening shift since he had come in so early. Dupont assured him that he had already made arrangements.

For her part, Burdy spent most of the morning roaming around Bayeux, window shopping. It wasn't like she could take any gifts back to anyone without giving away where she had been. She had warned Wheedin ahead of time that she would not call her long distance from Cousin Hota's in Colorado. It was too expensive. When Wheedin protested, Burdy reminded her that she didn't need a mother; *she* was the mother. So Wheedin backed off.

After lunch, Burdy took a nap. Clint offered to drive her to the cemetery, but Burdy decided to use the hotel shuttle service. She needed the solitude. She could see that Clint's feelings were hurt, but she promised to meet him for breakfast Saturday morning. Burdy didn't think she'd be up for a visit Friday night. Not after seeing Zeb.

She wore a navy skirt, red blouse, and white sweater. She also braided her hair, but instead of wrapping it about her head Pentecostal-style, she tied it off with a blue ribbon and pulled it over her right shoulder. A long strand of her mother's pearls completed the outfit. Next, she took the prayer stone from the bedside table and put it in her purse. Before leaving the room, Burdy took Hitty and put her in the purse too. The doll had been one of Maizee's most treasured possessions and she thought Zeb might want it. She dreaded that part of the conversation. It made her sick to her stomach to think of telling Zeb about Maizee.

As she waited in the hotel lobby for the shuttle, Burdy felt discombobulated. A mix of anger, frustration, and sorrow for everyone involved washed over her. She finally allowed that perhaps nothing good would come from this. Maybe she should have left well enough alone.

Chapter 36

Zeb was waiting right where he said he would be, under the Corsican pine near the stone wall. Burdy walked up to him, reached out her arms, and pulled him into a long, comforting embrace.

Neither said a word. They couldn't speak. They were both weeping.

A cool breeze blew in from the channel. The sky overhead was robin-egg blue with smears of white, brush-stroked clouds. A little girl wearing jeans, a green sweater, matching green shoes, and a flowered floppy hat ran through the rows of crosses. She was four, maybe five, only a little taller than the white marble crosses. A woman called after her: "*arrétez-vous et marchez*"—stop and walk. The child stopped in front of Burdy and Zeb, pointed at them, and called back to her mother: "*Maman, Pourquoi est-ce qu'ils pleurent?*"

Zeb pulled away from Burdy, wiped at his eyes, and said, "The little girl wants to know why we're crying."

Burdy turned toward the child and smiled. "It's okay, honey," she said. "These are happy tears."

Zeb draped his arm around his old friend and gave Burdy a tight side squeeze. He towered over her by a foot.

The young child's mother walked up and took her daughter's hand. "*Bonjour,*" she said, nodding. "*Pardon.*"

"*Bonjour,*" Zeb replied. He smiled and nodded in return.

Burdy opened her purse and pulled out a small package of tissues. "I knew I would be needing these," she said. She offered a couple to Zeb, who took them and blew his nose. Burdy laughed. "Some things never change. Your honk is as loud and obnoxious as ever."

"And I've see you're still as plainspoken as ever," Zeb said, laughing along with her.

"You didn't expect otherwise, did you?"

"No. I wouldn't even want otherwise."

"Well, let me look at you."

Zeb was the thinnest Burdy had ever seen him. Stringbean thin. He was already much taller than her, but being so skinny made him look even taller. He had aged, not just the ten years but more than that. His forehead was lined, and his mouth looked drawn into a perpetual worried expression. His eyes were hooded where they had never been before. Blue veins popped up on his neck and the tops of his hands. His Adam's apple was a protruding stone in his throat. Beyond the crinkles in his eyes, Burdy could still see the sweet boy that Zeb was once, but war and its aftermath had definitely taken its toll. Seeing him that way made her heart ache.

"Looking rough, ain't I?" Zeb said. He saw the truth of it in Burdy's eyes.

"I've seen you look better," Burdy admitted.

"Well, you are as pretty as a June rose in November," Zeb said. "You haven't aged a bit."

"Oh, c'mon now, Zeb. You know flattery will get you everywhere with me."

"I'm counting on it." Zeb looped his arm through Burdy's and led her away from the tree and the crosses toward the stone wall and the overlook of Omaha Beach. Burdy turned and looked back toward the cemetery.

"That's a sea of white crosses," she said.

"Over nine thousand. The bulk of them died during the D-Day landings and mission," Zeb replied. "Forty-five sets of brothers, most buried side by side."

"I can't even imagine it," Burdy said. She looked up at Zeb. He was facing the beach. She wondered where the worst of his memories were—in the cemetery behind him or on the beach in front of him. She was afraid to ask but did so anyway. "Did you come in at this beach?"

"No," Zeb said. "We landed south of here in a town called Sainte Mère Église. We had it bad but not nearly as bad as here." He reached for a cigarette, tapped one out for himself, and offered one to Burdy.

"No, thanks," she said. "I gave up tobacco."

"Good for you," Zeb said. "I wish I could." He struck a match to the cigarette and drew in a long breath until the end glowed red. "I guess I owe you an explanation."

"You don't owe me anything, Zeb. But I would like to know why you didn't come home. Why you let us go on thinking you were dead all this time." Burdy played with the strand of pearls around her neck. God's teardrops. That's what she'd always heard about pearls, that they were the tears God wept when he looked upon all the wrong that man had wrought.

Zeb heaved himself up on the wall, turned halfway toward the sea and halfway toward the crosses. He took a couple more long drags and then asked, "How is Maizee? How is my boy?"

It was Burdy's turn to avoid answers. "Rain is a right good kid, Zeb. He's doing great at school. He's learned to lip-read really well, and he recovered some of his hearing. It wasn't a total loss. He can talk with folks pretty good. He is so handsome, and the other kids at the Tennessee School for the Deaf really seem to have taken a shine to him, especially the girls." Burdy couldn't help rambling. She wanted to put off the inevitable, but she knew she couldn't stop it.

"And Maizee?" Zeb asked. "I reckon she's gone and remarried by now, huh? You can tell me, Burdy. I didn't expect she would stay single all this time, not thinking me dead and all. I hope she's happy. That's what's most important to me, that she's happy."

Burdy's stomach cinched up into a tight knot. It hadn't occurred to her that Zeb would have thought that Maizee remarried. But of course it made sense. What else would he think? Burdy leaned on the wall so she could face Zeb.

"There is no easy way to tell you this," she said, reaching over and putting her hand on Zeb's knee. "Maizee is dead, honey."

Zeb pinched the last of the cigarette between his fingers, took a final drag, then flicked it out towards the beach. He said nothing.

When she thought about it later, Burdy recalled how the lack of emotion from Zeb surprised her the most. How he didn't respond. How it seemed like he was just so used to hearing horrible news that nothing—not even the death of his beloved Maizee—shocked him anymore.

"You remember how sick she was with Rain?" Burdy continued. "How she kept hearing things, not sleeping and all? Well, it got worse when those government men came and told her you were missing and likely dead. She simply couldn't cope. I don't know what all was going through her head. I'm glad I don't know. If I knew, I might have done the same thing she did. Not long after them government men came, she took her own life, Zeb. I am so, so sorry to have to be the one to tell you."

Zeb stood up and offered his hand. He didn't ask any more questions. Burdy told Clint later that it was almost as if Zeb was deaf, as if he hadn't heard a single thing she said. He simply blocked out the entire conversation.

They walked back to the rows of crosses, moving slowly, stopping to read the names: Wilbur C. White, Clifford C. Tinsley, Seraphin J. Basille.

"Why are those ones different?" Burdy asked, pointing at a cluster.

"That's the Star of David," Zeb said. "For the Jewish men who died fighting."

Burdy walked up to one and read it aloud: "Jack Sonnenreich. 60th Infantry. 9th Division. New York. July 17, 1944."

"There are four women buried here as well," Zeb said.

"Really, women? I had no idea."

"Three of them were killed in the same jeep accident. They were all members of the first all-female, all-black battalion to serve overseas. They were known as the Six Triple Eight and had one of the most important jobs of all. They worked around the clock sorting the mail so that we could get our letters from home." Zeb shook his head. "You can't imagine how much it meant to us to get those letters."

"There's a lot about what you've seen and been through that I can't imagine," Burdy said.

"True. This fellow here is from Oklahoma: Robert J. Powers. June 6, 1944. 86th Squadron. 437th Troop Carrier."

"D-Day, huh?" Burdy said.

Zeb nodded. "My Sarge was from Oklahoma. He was married and had a couple of young sons. Sergeant Harootunian was a really good man. I liked him a lot. I trusted him. He was smart, too. He'd been around, seen some things. He was the last person I thought would die. I was with him when that happened."

"I am so sorry," Burdy said.

"You and me both." Zeb weaved slowly in and out between the crosses until they were standing before the cross belonging to Sargent Harootunian. Zeb's hands were stuffed into the pockets of his trousers. "It was the worst day of my life."

"Zeb, honey, you don't have to talk about it if you don't want to." Burdy was feeling a heaviness she had not known since Maizee's death. She was sorry she had come, sorry she was intruding on Zeb's memories. She knew better. Zeb was a good man. She should have known that something powerful, something awful, must have happened for him not to come back to his wife and son. She wanted to leave this place, this cemetery filled with broken bones and broken dreams. She wanted to get on that ship and sail far, far away from all of this. For the first time since she left

Christian Bend, Burdy couldn't wait to get back home. A person needs to know that some questions are better off unanswered.

But Zeb wasn't finished. "Sarge died trying to save me," he said. "I was hit in my leg. Right here." Zeb pointed at the fleshy part of his left thigh, right above the knee. "Harootunian pulled me into a hedgerow, looking for cover. He tied a tourniquet about my leg. The thing was, the leg wound was nothing, really. It burned like hellfire, but it wasn't worth Harootunian dying over. That's the thing. I was going to survive the leg. We both could have survived it, if only Harootunian hadn't been so damn set on helping me.

"Bastard Germans shot him in the back. He never saw it coming." Zeb paused, took a deep breath, exhaled. He clenched his jaw tight. He was determined to tell Burdy the story he had only told to one other person—Father Thom. The first time he told it was in the dark of the confession booth. Redemption is a hard thing to come by when you've killed people.

"I was next," Zeb said. "I should have died that day. I still don't know why I didn't. I've asked God why so many times that he's quit listening.

"I heard one of the Germans—there were two of them—say something to the other. I knew they intended to kill me. I was half outta my mind with rage. I started firing my own gun like a man gone mad on shine. One of the German's bullets hit my jaw, knocked out most of my teeth." Zeb slipped his tongue under his bottom dentures and lifted them so that Burdy could see.

"I thought I'd killed them both, but turns out I'd only killed one of them. The other bastard was shot in the back by a young French kid trying to help me. Part of the Resistance. Thing was, in my fury, I had shot at anything moving, and that included the kid. I killed him. He was just a kid, fourteen, fifteen maybe. I don't know for sure." Zeb reached over and grabbed Burdy by her shoulders. "Look at me! I am not a soldier. I don't deserve any honor. I am a killer! I shot a child dead!"

He was weeping now, and Burdy wept with him. Their sobs came forth in waves like those washing up on the shores of Omaha Beach. Relentless, unyielding, one swallowed up by the next one. Zeb's withered body heaved with grief, and Burdy pulled him into the tightest hug she could muster.

"Men and their damn wars," she said under her breath. She patted Zeb on the back, the way she had Rain so many times when he was a baby. "It's not your fault, Zeb. You have to know it's not your fault."

Zeb jerked back. "But don't you see? It is! It's all my fault. If it hadn't been for me, Sergeant Harootunian would be home watching his boys play college ball. That kid I killed? Who knows what good he would have brought into the world? And Maizee. My sweet, sweet Maizee. It's all my fault. All of it. I wished to God the bastard Germans had shot me dead that day before I ever even landed on the battlefield."

Burdy knew there was nothing she could say to make things any better for Zeb. He was wracked with a guilt she didn't know, could never know. Only those who had been to war, had killed another—had killed a child—would ever understand. Unsure of what else to do, Burdy prayed silently. *Please, Creator God, please help Zeb forgive himself.*

A man in a wheelchair rolled by; he was missing his legs from the knees down. He nodded at the two of them, grim-faced, as if to say, "I understand." Burdy wondered if Zeb might not be better off if he had lost a limb or two. There is a certain amount of empathy extended to soldiers who bear their wounds on the outside, an empathy not often afforded those who carry the silent wounds of survivor's guilt.

Burdy pulled the package of tissues from her purse again, took one, and handed all she had left to Zeb.

"I brought you something," she said. She took the prayer stone from her purse and placed it in his hands.

"An opal?" he said quietly, turning it over. "This has got to be the biggest one I've ever seen."

"It belonged to my great-grandfather" Burdy said. "It's been my personal prayer stone for years. Opals are sacred among my Cherokee ancestors."

"I can't accept this," Zeb said. He tried to place it back in Burdy's hands, but she refused.

"This is a stone of eternal hope," she said. "It will be good for your soul. It won't take away those bad memories, but it, along with prayer, will help set those memories right."

"Thank you, Burdy." Zeb doubted that anything could make his memories right again, but he knew Burdy gave him the stone out of love. He had expected Burdy to be angry with him. He thought she might have made the trip across the ocean just to give him a good lashing out. He knew she was sorely disappointed about him never coming home. How could she not be? But she had offered him nothing but love and mercy. It had been a long time since he felt as forgiven as Burdy made him feel in that moment. He put the stone in his pocket.

"I also brought you this," Burdy said. She handed Hitty to him.

"Maizee's doll?"

"Yes. She's a little worn after all these years, but I thought you might want something of Maizee's to hang on to. You can even sleep with her if you like."

Zeb ran his fingers over the doll's face and managed to muster a chuckle. "Burdy Luttrell, you are a mess."

"I suppose I am," she said. "I don't think that's ever going to change."

"And I love you for that," Zeb said.

He stopped outside the doorway to the cemetery's chapel and stepped aside to let Burdy enter first. She read the inscription carved into the wall: *Think not only of their passing. Remember the Glory of their Spirit.*

"Amen," she whispered. "Amen."

Chapter 37

Clint and Burdy spent Saturday poking around the Bayeux market, which stretched the entire length of downtown. There was indigo pottery and intricate lace, bright paintings and bottles of cider, delicate jewelry, and befuddling do-dads that caused Burdy to burst into laughter. She bought a small painting of Bayeux's charming Old Mill. Clint picked up some Gouda cheese, a couple loaves of fresh bread, wine, and a beautiful bouquet of pink and purple wildflowers for Burdy.

They spent the gloaming hour strolling through the cemetery of the British dead, lost in their own remembrances of war and its aftermath, and reading the inscriptions on the gravestones, which Burdy declared was like reading poetry.

"That's because a lot of these quotes are taken from poetry," Clint said.

"Well, that explains it then," Burdy said. She read aloud the next one she happened upon. "And in my heart, some late lark singing. Let me be gathered to the quiet west. Captain D. J. Ramsay. M. C. Scottish Horse. June 17, 1944. Age 28."

While rosebushes grew around many of the other graves, dandelions covered the ground around Captain Ramsay's headstone. Burdy bent over and pulled up the weeds.

"I can't help but wonder about who this young man was, what his family was like, and what dreams died along with him," she said. "Did he have a wife and children? Or did he leave behind a girlfriend who mourns their lost love still? What of his brothers and sisters, if he had any? Do they still tell stories of their childhood with him and laugh at the memories? Or has everyone simply forgotten him by now?"

Standing three gravestones over, Clint replied, "I think this one answers your last question." He read aloud from the inscription before him. "Not just one day, but every day we remember. Love, Mother, Dad and Charlie."

An intimate dinner at Clint's home capped off Burdy's last night in Bayeux. They ate the Gouda and bread and drank two bottles of wine. Both of them laughed too loudly at stories from their childhood. Burdy told of the time a piglet grabbed a mouthful of her hair and wouldn't let go, so Burdy, about six years old, retaliated by biting the piglet's foot until it squealed, and even then she wouldn't let up.

"One minute the piglet was swinging from my hair, and the next I was swinging the screaming piglet from my mouth," Burdy said.

Clint wiped tears of laughter from the corners of his eyes and took a deep breath. He reached over and put his hand on Burdy's. They kissed there over the leftover dinner plates and empty wineglasses, and later, exhausted from their lovemaking, slept curled around one another.

Sunday morning, Burdy packed in a hurry, tossing rather than neatly folding her things into the suitcases, then checking out of the Hotel Churchill before rushing off to join Clint and Zeb for Mass at the Bayeux Cathedral. Burdy took cues from the two men on when to stand, when to sing, when to kneel, and when to pray. She didn't understand most of what Father Thom was saying, although she knew that the homily was about forgiveness. She was reminded of something Preacher Blount once said: "When we fail in forgiveness, we condemn ourselves to being judged by our own standards."

Burdy had come to France with the intention of holding Zeb accountable to her standards. She came expecting, at least in part, to punish Zeb for abandoning Maizee and Rain. She'd failed to realize that what looked like abandonment was actually protection, at least

156

in Zeb's mind. He could not have returned to the hero's welcome in Christian Bend, not after what he had done. How would his neighbors there respond if they knew he'd shot and killed a boy? Coming to France taught Burdy that forgiveness requires context, while judgment rarely takes context into consideration.

Before heading off to Paris with Clint, Burdy gave Zeb one long embrace that conveyed the forgiveness she felt at that moment. "One day, I'll explain all this to Rain," she said. "I'll tell him what a good daddy you were."

"Thank you, Burdy," Zeb said. He was weeping now, at the mention of his son. "I hope Rain will find it in his heart to forgive me someday."

"I hope you learn to forgive yourself," Burdy whispered.

"I'm working on it." Zeb kissed the top of Burdy's forehead. "Bye-bye, Burdy."

Clint and Burdy arrived at Stacey and Jack's place late on Sunday. They all ate a light dinner on the balcony of the Hoyts' penthouse on Saint-Germain-des-Prés. Afterwards they walked the neighborhood, and Burdy stopped before a bright blue stove in a big picture window.

"That looks like the wood-burning stove at my friend Leela's house," she said. "Look, it has the silver handles on the doors and everything. Just like Leela's, except I've never seen one come in anything but cast-iron black."

"My grandmother had one, too," Stacey said. "I never understood how a person could get the temperature right for baking. I don't know how to work a stove that doesn't come with knobs to turn or buttons to push."

"Practice," Burdy said. "Lots of trial and error."

On Monday, the couples toured Notre Dame Cathedral, took a short trip down the River Seine. They stopped at a café, and

Burdy and Stacey shared a pink *macaron* while the men drank dark espresso.

"This is the most heavenly thing I've ever tasted," Burdy said. "Sort of like divinity in a much more melt-in-your-mouth way." Stacey laughed as she greedily popped the last bite into her mouth.

Afterwards, they walked over to the Eiffel Tower and posed for photos. Stacey promised to mail them to Burdy. The day ended with a hurried stroll through part of the Louvre.

"At the outbreak of the war, most of the collections here were evacuated," Jack said. He moved to the side so Burdy and Clint could get a closer look at Eugene Delacroix's *Liberty Leading the People*. "They were first moved to the Château de Chambord in the Loire valley, but as the war went on they were moved to other hiding places. Destroying the art of a country is one of the primary ways to erase its identity, and Hitler was all about that."

"Did you know that the boy holding a gun up on the right is sometimes thought to be an inspiration of the Gavroche character in Victor Hugo's book, *Les Misérables*?" Clint asked.

"I did not know that," Stacey said. "I loved that book. Have you read it, Burdy?"

"No." There was a weariness in Burdy's voice. She had seen and done so much in the few weeks she had been away from home. In the Bend, she was used to taking time each evening to ponder her day's experiences and encounters. She was looking forward to getting home and sitting on the porch and watching the sun set over the hills. She missed the girls. She had hired the Campbell kids to look after the chickens while she was away and knew that they were well cared for, but she still couldn't help worrying about them. She wondered if the events of the past three weeks would soon seem like a dream to her.

"Well, you must," Stacey said, clasping Burdy's hand. "Then you must write and tell me about what you think of it, promise?"

"I'm not sure they'll have it at the Rogersville library."

"No worries. I will loan you my copy for your trip home," Stacey said. She slipped her foot out of a red heel she was wearing. "These shoes are killing me. I think I'm about done for the day."

"We can go," Jack said.

"I hate it because we've hardly even begun to show Burdy all the wonderful works here," Stacey said. "I'm sorry. I should have worn more comfortable shoes."

"Don't worry about it," Burdy said. "I'm worn out, too, and I have a big day ahead of me tomorrow."

"What time does your ship leave?" Jack asked.

"I think I have to board at 7 p.m."

"Well, you are just going to have to promise to come back," Stacey said. "We need at least two weeks to show you around Paris properly. It is simply impossible to see Paris in a day or two."

"Yes," Jack said. "You must promise to return as soon as you can. Isn't that right, Clint?" He winked at his friend.

"I'd like that very much," Clint said, giving Burdy's waist a tight squeeze.

"Perhaps," Burdy said, "if you all insist."

On Burdy's last day in Paris, Clint took her to the Jardin de Luxembourg, where they strolled the grounds, lingered around the Medici Fountain, and looked on wistfully as children floated brightly colored miniature sailboats at the Grand Basin.

"When I was a little girl, I imagined I was a queen and had a whole village of little people. People so little they could all fit on one of those boats," Burdy said.

"Were you a good queen or a bad queen?" Clint asked.

"I was a very kindly queen. All the little people loved me."

"I am sure they did," Clint said, laughing. "All the big people love you now."

Pulling her in close, Clint kissed Burdy. His full lips were wet and soft, and she didn't want the kiss to end. She felt a growing ache in her chest, an unspoken awareness that wished for time to stop. She did not want to get on that ship in Le Havre. She did not want to return to her life in the Bend. She wanted to stay right where she was—in Clint's arms.

They ate lunch at the nearby Café Tournon, where Burdy had her first bite of goose liver. She didn't have the nerve to tell Clint that she much preferred chicken livers, fried. But that dessert? Burdy told Clint she could eat half a dozen more of those little chocolate cakes with the warm, pudding-like middle.

"Go ahead," he said, motioning for the waitress. A young woman wearing bright red lipstick began clearing their plates. "*Onze plus de chocolat mi-cuit s'il vous plait,*" Clint said.

"*Tout de suite, monsieur,*" the waitress replied.

"Don't you dare!" Burdy scolded. "I was only kidding."

"*Êtes-vous sûrs?*" the waitress asked, winking at Clint.

"*Oui,*" Clint replied. He handed her 500 Francs and told her to keep the change.

"*Merci, monsieur.*"

Afterwards, Clint drove Burdy to Le Havre. They were both quiet on the drive, neither willing to say what worried them both— that they might never see one another again.

Clint carried Burdy's suitcases aboard the ship and made sure she was settled in before taking his leave. Burdy felt like a well-seasoned traveler, completely confident about the journey home. Saying good-bye to Clint was another matter.

"I am not the same woman I was when I left Christian Bend," she told him. She wrapped her arms around his neck as they stood nose to nose, whispering their farewell. "France has changed me."

"*All changes, even the most longed for, have their melancholy; for what we leave behind us is a part of ourselves; we must die to one life before we can enter another,*" Clint said.

"*We must die to one life before we can enter another,*" Burdy repeated. "That's beautiful, and so perfect. What a smart man you are."

"Not my words," Clint said, his voice heavy with sadness. "I'm quoting a Frenchman far more brilliant than me—Anatole France. Poet. Journalist. Novelist."

"Well, you are smart enough to put his words to memory," Burdy said. "And it is true that what I am leaving behind is a part of myself."

"I know," Clint said. "I am going to miss you, *ma moitié*. I don't know when I have laughed as much or felt as deeply as I have in these past few days with you. I think I shall become like that piglet, refusing to let go of you."

"What is that you called me? Ma what?"

"*Ma moitié?*"

"Yes. What does it mean?"

"My half."

Part III

1987

Chapter 38

Burdy had a fitful night at the hospital, tossing, turning, carrying on. She kept calling out for somebody Wheedin didn't know. On Saturday morning, Wheedin asked everybody if they knew who this "Clint" fella was that her momma called after. Nobody knew anybody in the Bend or even uptown with the name "Clint."

"Maybe she was talking about Clinton, the town," Doc said. "It's not too far from here."

"I don't think so," Wheedin said. "She said some stuff I never imagined my momma saying."

"What kind of stuff?" Leela asked.

"The kind of things you might say to somebody you are intimate with," Wheedin replied.

"Oh my gracious," Leela said.

Rain was sitting in his usual chair near the end of the bed, lip-reading the conversation between the womenfolk, and thankful for once that he could blame his lack of commentary on his partial deafness.

"It must be the drugs and the dementia still," Doc reasoned. "Far as any of us at the Bend knew, your momma hasn't been with any man other than your daddy. I certainly never heard tell of her being with anybody."

"You don't think she could have been involved with one of those men she cared for at Pressmen's Home, do you?" Wheedin asked.

"Not far as I knew," Doc said.

Nobody was paying any attention when Burdy opened her eyes and looked around the room. She had heard every bit of the conversation. Smiling, she thought, *What they don't know won't hurt them none. A woman don't have to tell everything she knows and does.*

She had kept her relationship with Clint a secret for a very long time, and she intended to go to her grave with it.

Not that she was ready for the bone pit just yet, mind you. She had taken a bad hit, no question about it, but she had survived. And if there was one lesson she'd learned during her visits with Zeb over the years, it was never to ask why. Why can be such a useless question. Instead, Burdy had learned that it was best to ask God, "What now?"

She had a pretty clear idea of what God wanted her to do anyhow. She didn't even need to even ask about that.

"What's a woman got to do to get some ham and eggs around here?" Burdy said.

Everybody in the room turned toward her, gap-mouthed, disbelieving.

"Momma!" Wheedin cried. She grabbed hold of Burdy's hand and leaned in so close that Burdy could smell the Juicy Fruit gum she was chewing. "Do you know who I am?"

"Lord, child, I give birth to you. I should hope to shout I know who you are. What is wrong with you?" Burdy was clearly annoyed. "Sit me up, would you?"

Doc pushed the button to raise the bed.

"What day is it?" Burdy asked.

"Saturday," Leela said.

Rain moved from the chair to Burdy's side. He reached down and patted her forearm. "Good to see you, Burdy," he said. People unaccustomed to Rain's halting way of talking had to listen carefully to make out his words, but everybody gathered around Burdy's bed understood him well enough.

"Good to see you, too, Rain. But what are you doing here? Aren't you supposed to be off in Yankee territory in Rhode Island?"

Burdy pointed to a glass of water on a nearby tray. "Hand me that, would you, please?"

Rain passed the cup to Burdy. She took a long sip, and another, and then studied herself. Her leg was wrapped in bandages from the kneecap up, and an IV drip ran into her right hand. She was a little woozy, but otherwise she felt okay, considering. Still, she wasn't up for dancing a jig, that was for darn sure.

"Did they all die?" she asked.

Wheedin looked at Leela, who looked at Doc, who looked at Burdy.

"Did all who die, Momma?" Wheedin asked.

"Those other people who got shot yesterday at Laidlow's?"

"Momma, the shooting wasn't yesterday. You've been in the hospital a week now. The shooting was last Friday."

Wheedin was worried. Her momma was so disoriented. She seemed to have lost all track of time. "Do you remember the shooting?"

"Listen here, Wheedin Luttrell, it is not every day a woman walks into the pharmacy and is carried out on a stretcher and loaded onto a helicopter. A person tends to remember the big moments of her life. Getting shot ranks right up there with my idea of a big life moment. Of course I remember it! Why are you treating me like I'm a few fish short of a string?" Burdy's tone was sharp, commanding.

Doc chuckled to himself. He was the only person in the room who sensed that whatever dementia problem Burdy experienced as a result of the trauma and surgery was temporary. She was back to her old self for sure.

"They died, didn't they? All of them?"

"Yes, Momma. They did." Wheedin hated telling the truth, but she couldn't bring herself to lie. Burdy was bound to find out sooner or later. "But they caught the fellow who done the killing."

"They did?" Burdy said, surprised.

"Yes, ma'am," Wheedin said. "It was in the paper yesterday morning. Officer Hal Evans with the Bean Station Police Department."

"The police officer did the shooting?" Burdy asked.

"Uh-huh," Wheedin said, nodding. "He'd been on some sort of medical disability."

"Lord, what is this world coming to when the police are the ones going around shooting at innocent people?" Burdy said. She tried to scooch herself up in the bed but let out a holler. Her leg was hurting something fierce.

"Try and relax, Momma," Wheedin said. "You've been through a lot. I'll call the nurse and have her get the doctor in here soon as possible." She reached for the nurse call remote, but Burdy grabbed it away from her.

"You'll do no such thing!" she said. "I don't need a doctor in here right now. In fact, I don't need any of you in here right now. Get on out. All y'all. Except for Rain. I need to speak to Rain. Alone."

"I don't think that's a good idea, Momma. You need your rest." Wheedin reached for the call remote again. Burdy slapped her hand.

"You've just told me that I've been asleep for a week," Burdy said. Her cheeks were flushed. Her leg was hurting. She could use a dose of pain medication, but she was intent on not taking anything that would put her back to sleep, even for a few hours, before she spoke with Rain. "Please leave. Please?"

Doc walked over and whispered to Wheedin. "I think we ought to do as your momma asks."

"You do?"

"Yes. She'll be fine. We'll be right outside the door if she needs anything. C'mon, honey. She's set her mind to this, and you know how she can be when you cross her. There's no reason to upset her right now."

"You better listen to him," Burdy said. There was nothing wrong with her hearing. Doc had been speaking quietly, and Burdy heard every word.

"Alright, Momma," Wheedin said. "Rain, we will be right outside the room if you need anything."

"Okay," Rain said.

Wheedin, Doc, and Leela left the room and shut the door behind them.

Burdy put down the call remote and reached for Rain's hand. "Come in closer, son. I got something important to say to you."

Rain leaned down close to Burdy and kissed her cheek. She returned the kiss with one of her own.

Silently, Rain noted that Burdy smelled old, the way everybody smells when they've been in a hospital bed for days on end. She needed a shower and a good hair washing. He made a mental note to tell Wheedin.

"Oh, Rain, I fear you might think I've just given you a Judas kiss."

Rain had no idea what Burdy was talking about. He wasn't sure she knew what she was talking about, but he decided to play along, no matter how crazy she might get. He would smile and nod and generally give her all the affirmations she needed. There was no need to upset her.

"I owe you an apology," Burdy said. "I've been keeping something from you all these years. I meant to tell you. Honest, I did. It's just, well, it's complicated."

Rain didn't know whether to keep listening or to get Wheedin. He could tell by the animated way Burdy was talking that she was getting more and more agitated. He put his hand in the air and lowered it, like he was pressing on something, while he kept repeating, "Okay. Okay. Okay."

Burdy shook her head. "It's not okay. It's not okay at all, Rain. I could have died in that pharmacy shooting, and you would have never known because I failed to tell you."

"Failed to tell me what?" Rain repeated. "What is it I don't know, Burdy?"

"It's your daddy, Rain. Your daddy Zeb. He's alive. In France, and I've seen him."

Rain was sure Burdy was delusional now. He reached for the cup of water. "Calm down. You're getting too worked up. Here." Rain put the water up to Burdy's lips, but she pushed the cup away.

"I don't want any damn water, Rain! I'm trying to tell you— your daddy is alive!"

Burdy was yelling so loudly that Wheedin and Doc and Leela could hear her out in the hallway.

"Did I just hear Momma tell Rain his daddy is alive?" Wheedin asked.

"That's what it sounded like to me," Doc said.

"That's what I heard," Leela said.

Wheedin opened the door and walked into the room. Doc and Leela followed. Rain looked up, and Wheedin saw the fear in his eyes.

"Burdy," Doc said. He walked over to the bed and rubbed the frowns from her forehead. "Take a deep breath, honey. Everything is going to be alright."

"It will be as soon as I get the hell out of this place and you all quit treating me like I'm not right in the head. I'm trying to tell Rain that his daddy is alive and well in France. I've been there, several times actually."

"We believe you, honey," Leela said. She stood beside Doc, grasping the bedrail. "But you need some rest."

It was clear to Burdy that Leela didn't believe her one little bit.

"Momma," Wheedin said, "if you don't calm down, I'm going to get the doctor right now and drag him in here myself."

170

"Fine, go get him. I don't give a care," Burdy said. Turning to Rain, she made one last pitch. "Go to my house. In the back of the bottom dresser drawer in my bedroom, underneath Tibbis's old flannel pajamas, is a blue velvet box, about yay big." She spread her hands apart to indicate the size of a cigar box. "Inside that box are all the letters I've gotten from your daddy over the years. You'll also find the travel receipts of all the trips I've made to France over the years."

"Okay," Rain said. "I will look."

"You promise?" Burdy said.

"Yes. I promise." He made the sign of a cross over his heart.

"Okay, good. You'll see. I'm not talking out of my head." Burdy glared at Wheedin. "No matter what some folks in this room might think, I was not shot in the head, Missy."

"I never said you were, Momma."

"Well then, quit treating me like I don't know what I'm talking about. And go get me something to eat, would you? I'm so hungry I could gnaw the leg off of Preacher Blount."

Everybody in the room laughed. Wheedin headed to the nurse station to order her momma some food. Doc and Leela hung around until an orderly brought in a tray of scrambled eggs, grits, a bowl of peaches, and a carton of milk.

"We're going to head on back home for now," Doc said as Burdy sliced open the biscuit and slathered it with butter. "Wheedin will keep us up to date."

"I'm sure she will," Burdy said.

"We'll be back on Monday or Tuesday," Doc said.

"Don't bother," Burdy said. "I plan on springing this joint first thing Monday morning."

"Now, Momma," Wheedin interrupted. "Don't be making any plans until we've spoken with the doctor."

Burdy rolled her eyes.

Rain followed Doc and Leela out into the hallway. "Any chance I could get a ride up to the Bend with you?" he asked.

"Why, sure," Doc said. "We would love for you to come home with us."

"Thank you," Rain said. "I know Burdy was talking out of her head, but I want to keep good on the promise I made her."

Chapter 39

On Sunday, while Leela and Doc were taking their usual afternoon nap between church services, Rain walked over to Burdy's house. He took the key from the rusted Prince Albert tobacco can Burdy kept high on a shelf on the back porch.

There was a time when Burdy left her doors unlocked all day and all night, and nobody ever even thought about busting in her home and stealing anything. Everybody in the Bend used to leave their homes unlocked. Not anymore. Not since marijuana replaced tobacco as the cash crop for the region. Now, people had to lock up.

Rain unlocked the door and walked inside. The house had that same funky smell it had when he was a little boy—lemon polish and licorice root. Burdy used the root to cure everything from a sore throat to arthritis, both common ailments around these parts.

Even though it was the middle of the afternoon, the house was dark. Ida Mosely had come in to draw the curtains closed and pull the shades. Sunlight cast an outline of the windows onto the woven oval rug in the living room. Rain hadn't thought to ask Burdy if she wanted him to bring her anything from home. He should have done that. She probably could have used some of her own clothes, her Bible maybe, but, truth be known, he didn't want Burdy to know he was going to her house.

Rain figured it would create more problems for Wheedin if Burdy knew he had been to her home and didn't find the letters she swore she had. And he was pretty darn sure he wasn't going to find any such box.

Where did she say it was? He remembered: in her bedroom, the bottom dresser drawer. Rain felt like he was trespassing, walking into Burdy's bedroom. He'd been in this home hundreds of times over the years, and not once had he been into this room.

To his right, a pink chenille bedspread covered the bed. A hurricane lamp sat on the end table. A pine dresser with varnish as thick as honey was pushed up against the far wall.

Several silver-framed photos were spread across the top of the dresser. The largest picture was of a young Burdy and Tibbis holding Wheedin. Even as a chubby baby, Wheedin had a headful of coal-black hair. She had so much hair it looked fake, like somebody had glued a toupee to the top of her little baby head. There was a photo of Rain and Burdy hugging each other, taken right after his high school graduation. And a picture of his momma and his daddy that he'd never seen before.

It was a small photo. A pregnant Maizee was holding up a string of fish and appeared to be letting out a belly laugh. Only the left side of Zeb's face showed because he was turned looking at Maizee. Rain held the photo closer and studied his dad's expression. Zeb wasn't displaying a hint of envy over his wife's catch. The smile on his face revealed nothing but pure devotion and admiration. Zeb was proud for Maizee. Rain winced. He wished what he had wished all his life—that he'd been able to get to know his parents the way Burdy had, the way Doc and Leela had.

He put the photo back, then knelt down and opened the drawer. Burdy said the box was somewhere in the back. Rain was loath to rummage through a woman's dresser drawer, but thankfully, there didn't appear to be anything too delicate here. Mostly Burdy's nightgowns, some socks in the corner wadded over one another, and a stack of flannel shirts, Tibbis's probably.

Rain reached in and began feeling his way through the folded clothes. He took hold of something hard and square. It wasn't thick enough to be the box Burdy described. Rain lifted it up.

He slipped the object out of an embroidered pillowcase and saw a high school diploma awarded to one Burdy Luttrell. It had a golden seal and the date, June 16, 1951. Rain smiled. That woman was full of surprises. Rain had always assumed that, like a lot of other people in the Bend, Burdy hadn't finished high school. Apparently, she had obtained her degree sometime in the years following his parents' death. Well, good for her. Rain placed the diploma back into the pillowcase and hid it back underneath the gowns.

A squirrel ran through the gutter outside the bedroom window. Rain jumped. "Men have no business going through a woman's things," he said, talking to himself. But he was too far in to stop now. He reached to the very back and felt along the bottom of the drawer. There was nothing on the right side and nothing on the left, but he felt something in the middle. Something soft. Grabbing hold of it, he pulled out the blue velvet box Burdy had told him he would find.

Grasping it, Rain stood up, his hands sweaty and trembling. He was afraid to open the lid. Afraid for Burdy and afraid for himself. If the letters weren't there, then Burdy was suffering some sort of serious dementia. If the letters were there, that meant Burdy was telling the truth. He couldn't even consider what the truth would mean.

Rain took in a deep breath, held it, and exhaled.

"Oh, sweet Jesus," he muttered when he opened the lid and saw a stack of yellowed envelopes. He read the postmark of the top letter: Bayeux, France. And he knew without reading a word that they were the letters from his father.

THE END

175

Acknowledgments

Not far from Basel, Switzerland, is the charming German community of Kandern. Up on a scenic hillside near an ancient cistern is The Art Factory (artfactorykandern.com), a place where artists and creators gather to encourage imagination.

Rick and Mary Beth Holladay are the hosts and visionaries behind The Art Factory. I met Rick when we were students at Oregon State University. He was studying art, and I was studying communications. On a Friday night in October 1978, Rick introduced me to Tim, the man who would become my husband.

Over the years, Rick and Mary Beth have invited us to visit. During the summer of 2013, we accepted their invitation. While Tim and Rick worked on projects around the factory, and Mary Beth served as a gracious host to dozens of artists coming and going, I taught a workshop on writing and worked on *Burdy*. Thank you, Rick and Mary Beth, for being such fun-loving and thoughtful hosts and for giving me a place to write, think, imagine, and create.

Another chance meeting led me to the town of Bayeux, France. Michael Ross Harper, who is part-owner of the fabulous Fiddleheads gift store in Columbus, Georgia, told me about Bayeux. "You must go there," he insisted. I will forever be indebted to Ross for his recommendation. I fell in love with Bayeux and with all of Normandy. I hope somebody in France reads this story and invites me to visit again soon.

As for my friends at Mercer University Press, you all are the hardest-working bunch of people in publishing. You do your jobs with unflinching devotion and unyielding humor. I adore all of you—Mary Beth Kosowski, Marsha Luttrell (no relation to Burdy),

Marc Jolley, Candice Morris, and Jenny Toole. I thank my lucky Oregon stars for you.

Kelley Fuller Land took a polishing rag to this manuscript and gave it a military-style spit-shine. Thank you, Kelley. Burdy's story is so much better because of the work you do. Thank you for your keen eye and insightful heart.

Hugs and thanks to Joyce Christian for inviting me to the 2014 Christian family reunion in Christian Bend, Tennessee. And many thanks to all the Christians in Christian Bend who remember Aunt Lucille Christian and have shared stories and photos of her with me. Cil is the inspiration for Burdy. An extra big hug to the Christian kin who gave me the photo of Aunt Cil.

Thank you to Darnell Arnoult for inviting me to conduct a writing workshop at the Heritage Mountain Literary Festival at Lincoln Memorial University in Harrogate, Tennessee. Darnell, I learned a great deal from my time at LMU.

Thank you to Tina Prochaska and Judi Brookshire for inviting me to tour Tennessee School for the Deaf in Knoxville. And for your insights on living deaf in a hearing world.

Thank you Zack Sinner for helping me sort through Burdy's medical issues. Your advice was valuable.

To the friends and family who hosted me during the writing of this work—Charlie and Ann Marie Harootunian, Raymond and Annis Spears, Jerry and Patti Burke, Ken and Sherri Callaway, David and Jane Wilson—thank you.

And to you, dear readers, who have bought my books, written reviews, and shared my work online or over coffee, thank you for believing in me, praying for me, and for loving Burdy. I write with you all sitting in the room alongside me.

Thom Chambliss, Wanda Jewell, and indie booksellers, who stock my work and encourage readers to read it, *merci beaucoup*.

Sullivan, I am delighted every time you greet me with "Books?" and run to grab one. I hope you will share your love of reading with your cousin Sawyer and your baby brother.

And lastly, to the families of those who suffer from post-traumatic stress disorder, whatever the cause, there is healing in telling your stories. I pray that you will find somebody who will listen. If you are a veteran, or the family of a veteran, I recommend connecting with Disabled American Veterans (dav.org). They are there to serve those who have served.

Discussion Questions for Book Clubs

1. If you read *Mother of Rain*, were you surprised to discover that Zeb was alive in *Burdy*?

2. The debates within the deaf community around the use of cochlear implants have been heated and fierce, yet YouTube videos of children hearing for the first time often go viral. What are your thoughts about these implants?

3. Many of the advances in technology that we use today—text messaging, FaceTime, and others—have long been employed in more rudimentary forms by the deaf community. Can you think of other ways that the hearing world benefits from the deaf community?

4. Burdy travels to France aboard the *SS United States*, one of the fastest ocean liners of its time. Have you ever traveled via an ocean liner? What did you like/dislike about your trip?

5. Drastic changes have taken place in Appalachia in the course of the past fifty years. Some of those changes are reflected in *Burdy*. What changes do you see in her character?

6. Hitty doesn't seem to hold any power over Burdy the way she did with Maizee. Why do you think that is?

7. In France, Burdy develops a love interest. Do you think Burdy had to get away from the Bend in order to find love again? Why or why not?

8. Burdy hides the fact that she got an education. Why might a woman of her place and time do that?

9. Burdy goes to France with the intention of holding Zeb accountable, but she ends up extending forgiveness to him. Why did she change her mind?

10. Zeb has injuries that keep him from returning home, but his injuries aren't on the outside. He is suffering from post-traumatic stress disorder, more commonly referred to as PTSD. You don't have to be a war survivor to experience this disorder; it can be the result of any trauma. Have you or someone you know dealt with PTSD? What are some of the challenges it poses?

11. Burdy intends to tell Rain about finding his father. Why do you think she waited so long to follow through on that?

12. Burdy keeps her relationship with Clint a secret. Why do you think she does this?

13. Wheedin assumes that her mother is suffering from dementia when she finally tells Rain about his father. This is likely due to Burdy's age. Is this age discrimination? Have you ever witnessed or personally faced age discrimination?

14. Burdy has a prayer stone, a sacred stone, that came from a great-grandfather. She takes it to France and leaves it with Zeb. Do you have a physical item that connects you to your ancestors and to God?

15. Rain found the letters Burdy said he would find. What do you think he will do next? What would you do if you discovered such news?

Contact the Author

Karen loves to hear from readers. She is available to speak to book clubs. You can contact her at her website at karenzach.com, via Twitter @karenzach, or find her on Facebook.